Margaret Yorke lives in Buckinghamshire. She is the recipient of the 1999 Cartier Diamond Dagger Award and is a past chairman of the Crime Writers' Association. In 1982 she won the Swedish Academy of Detection Award for the best crime novel in translation.

MARGARET YORKE

No Medals for the Major

WARNER BOOKS

A *Warner Futura* Book

First published in Great Britain in 1974 by Geoffrey Bles
Published by Arrow Books in 1981

This edition published by Warner Futura in 1995
Reprinted 1996, 1999

Copyright © Margaret Yorke 1974

The moral right of the author has been asserted.

A CIP catalogue record for this book
is available from the British Library.

ISBN 0 7515 1193 5

Printed in England by Clays Ltd, St Ives plc

Warner
A Division of
Little, Brown and Company (UK)
Brettenham House
Lancaster Place
London WC2E 7EN

No Medals for the Major

PART ONE

I

MAJOR JOHNSON closed the front door of his bungalow and tested the lock. He paused on the porch and surveyed with pride the small, shaven front lawn with its fringe of antirrhinums. Over his head hung a wooden sign bearing the single word *Tobruk* carved in poker-work; a faint smell of varnish came from it, for the major had just given it a fresh coat.

The day was warm and humid, and the sun shone down on the major as he strode forth into the village street. He stepped out with a light tread, for he was going to Fleckington, and his mind dwelt fondly on the charms of Miss Mainwaring, the town's librarian, whom he planned to invite to lunch with him at The Feathers.

Though today feeling young in heart, Major Johnson was in fact fifty-eight years old, a short man, stockily built, with wisps of grey hair around a bald dome and a neatly trimmed moustache. At the close of his military career he had come to live in Wiveldown, where property was cheaper than in areas nearer cities or the coast. He had bought the bungalow with his gratuity and his savings, and had spent happy months doing it up, profiting from all he had learned about home maintenance on his army resettlement course.

He had met Miss Mainwaring when, ignorant of what to plant in the garden round his new home, he had gone in search of helpful books; she had led him past horticulture to other pleasures, and a book about Java and the memoirs of a general were due to be returned today. Not much of a reader until he retired, he now made constant forays into new worlds, and the chief delight of this fresh interest was discussing what he had read with Miss Mainwaring afterwards.

'Not got your car today, then, Major Johnson?' asked a woman as he boarded the bus behind her.

It was Deirdre Flint, one of the sisters who ran the post office, taking time off to go to market, for Thursday was market day in Fleckington.

'It's having a new gear-box fitted. I'm fetching it this morning,' Major Johnson said. He found Mrs Flint, with her jet-black hair and aggressive bosom, alarming in the post office, but out here among other travellers she did not seem so formidable. 'Lovely morning, isn't it?' he added.

'It'll rain by night-time, mark my words,' said Mrs Flint.

'My runner beans need rain,' said Major Johnson. He waited for Mrs Flint to stow herself and her baskets in one seat, and took another across the gangway so that they might converse without physical proximity.

'Farmers don't,' said someone sitting in front of Mrs Flint, who now leaned forward to talk to this other acquaintance.

Major Johnson sat back, relieved to be spared a dialogue with Mrs Flint throughout the journey, but pleased with their small interchange; he was beginning to mingle.

Seated high in the bus, the outlook was different from when he drove to town in his dark green Morris 1300. He had a good view of the village as they passed the last cottages and a gaunt Victorian villa, *The Hollies*, set back at the end of a long drive, behind a wilderness of shrubs. Then there were fields for some miles before they reached the outskirts of Fleckington.

It had begun in the library, but Major Johnson's friendship with Miss Mainwaring was not confined to the realm of books, for they had met at cookery classes all last winter. When he saw a notice about them in the library, he had consulted her about his suitability as a pupil. A bachelor, he had lived in barracks as a young man, and after he was commissioned in the mess, so that beyond simple fry-ups and opening tins, he was no great cook. Miss Mainwaring had reassured him. She would be at the classes too and would shepherd him along. Thus encouraged, he enrolled, and was not the only man to do so; the class included a widowed schoolmaster, a man whose wife was in a wheelchair, and an enthusiastic schoolboy.

The tutor, Mrs Fellowes, a large woman with a commanding manner, placed Major Johnson and Miss Mainwaring at adjoining tables, and so their acquaintance grew from week to week until summer came and the course ended.

With the bungalow painted, the garden tamed, and some finer elements of cooking mastered, Major Johnson had time on his hands and realised that he was lonely. So, slowly, he made his decision: there was still time to marry. Older people did it every day.

It was to Miss Mainwaring, of course, that he planned, after a careful campaign, to offer his hand. She seemed kind; and though not pretty, she had a pleasant face; her curly brown hair was only lightly flecked with grey, and above all, she was small. Beside her, Major Johnson forgot that so was he. Now that youth was past, she would not look for ardour in a suitor, and he would proceed slowly, in order not to alarm her. Companionship was what he sought, no more; most of the time he successfully banished thoughts of wrapping his arms around Miss Mainwaring's neat form.

Once, as a young man, he had been in love, but the girl had married another man, and though he had always hoped to find someone else, it had not happened. He had moved about the world so much that there never seemed to be time, and then, somehow, the years ran out. The other officers in the mess grew younger and younger; they called him Uncle Fred and invented a giddy past for him. When he heard about their conquests he knew he could not compete. He sank gradually into his bachelor role, useful at dinner parties and even sometimes baby-sitting. Now all that was gone, and he was adrift in an unfamiliar society.

At first, after he retired, he planned to get some sort of job, but the only suitable one he could find was that of time-keeper in a paint factory in Fleckington. After he had straightened up the bungalow he worked there for some months, but he made no

9

real friends. He decided to leave and seek something with more human contact; then came the cookery lessons, and this summer he had spent five afternoons a week selling admission tickets at Chorlbury Manor, a local stately home. Miss Mainwaring had found him this job, for Admiral Bruce, the curator of the Manor, had asked her if she knew of anyone, so she was, in a sense, already his guardian angel.

Thus, with hope in his heart, he embarked upon his courtship.

II

Miss Celia Mainwaring had lived in Fleckington ever since her mother was widowed during the war. They were comfortable together. Celia did not bother much about housekeeping, for her mother's health was excellent until she died of a heart attack soon after Major Johnson came to Wiveldown. For years both ladies were members of an amateur orchestra, the mother playing the cello and the daughter the violin. Miss Mainwaring belonged to the dramatic society, and to a group dedicated to preserving the beauties of rural England, and she was captain of Fleckington's Ladies' Tennis Six. She did not enjoy sitting idly about, nor did she like to hear of anyone else just whiling time away, hence her interest in getting Major Johnson settled with his gardening and cooking; she had done the same for others in the past, though usually guiding men more towards woodwork than *haute cuisine*. She kept abreast of what was currently being published during library hours.

Her sister had been the pretty one; she had married young and now had four children to whom Celia was a rather bossy aunt. No one had ever asked her to marry them, nor did she expect that anyone ever would now. She seldom thought about it, for she was much too occupied.

She ran the library with the help of several part-time assistants whom she also saw out of office hours since some of their other interests overlapped. She was welcome in her friends' homes, for she was no threat to matrimonial safety and was always helpful in a crisis. She and her mother had entertained a lot, the mother cooking, and Celia laying the table, arranging the flowers and whipping the cream. Now, singlehanded, Celia found she lacked expertise and so she took the cooking lessons. Each winter, in any case, she followed two courses, one academically slanted such as German or the History of Art, the other recreational like the cooking; in this way she had learned to dressmake, model in clay, identify birds, and speak smatterings of several languages.

When Major Johnson, accepting from her Sir Arthur Grimble's *A Pattern of Islands*, invited her to lunch she was taken aback. Each time he left the library she forgot about him till they met again. She hesitated, something she rarely did, while the major hovered anxiously before her desk, holding up the queue of other readers waiting to change their books.

'Thank you. That would be nice,' she said, and pointed out to her friend Mavis later that it would have been difficult to refuse since she went to The Feathers nearly every day in any case.

Major Johnson had timed his visit to the library for a quarter to one, so that he could be there when it closed for lunch and thus escort her down the road. He read *Country Life* while he waited for her, then walked proudly at her side on the kerb edge of the pavement. The Feathers was busy, but the major, though small, had commanded men, even though they were mostly military clerks and not fighting troops. He found a corner table in the crowded bar, bought two sherries, and gave their order all with a minimum of fuss and a maximum of efficiency. Miss Mainwaring was quite impressed.

'There's Mrs Fellowes,' she said, when he sat down. 'Over there, near the window.'

'Oh yes,' said Major Johnson. Mrs Fellowes, the cookery tutor, had seen them and gave a slight wave in their direction. 'She lives in Wiveldown,' he added.

'Yes,' said Miss Mainwaring.

'Where I live,' Major Johnson said.

'Oh – do you?'

Why be cast down because she had forgotten? He thought of all the postcards she had sent him, telling him that certain books were waiting for him.

A flash of recollection came to Celia.

'Ah yes – *Tobruk*. That's the name of your house, isn't it? Were you there?'

'Yes,' he admitted, and was rewarded by the way Miss Mainwaring's blue eyes widened.

'What an experience,' she said.

Major Johnson did not tell her that his job had been not to fight, but to find supplies for those who did. He hoped she would not ask him about the siege; he might have to reveal the true nature of his role.

'I enjoy my job at Chorlbury Manor, the one you found for me,' he volunteered, to change the subject. 'I'd like to be a guide, if I could learn enough about the house to do it properly.'

'Why not?' asked Miss Mainwaring.

'Mrs Fellowes is a guide there. Did you know?'

Miss Mainwaring did.

'She's most capable. She's very good at answering difficult questions.'

'She's used to that. She teaches at the comprehensive school, part-time,' said Miss Mainwaring.

'Oh!'

Time flew. Major Johnson had rehearsed in advance some topics for discussion so that conversation would flow smoothly. He described his garden and suggested she might care to see it one day. She disclosed that she was going to Italy soon for her annual holiday. This dismayed the major, for it meant a delay in his programme, but he rallied. He had been stationed in Italy after the war and gave her tips on what to see. Miss Mainwaring had been to Italy six times already. She scarcely listened.

'I'll see you again before you go,' he said to her, resolving if need be to sit up half the night finishing the books she'd given him today.

She refused his offer to escort her back to the library. He

thought of asking her out for a drive in his car over the weekend, if he could find a time to suit her when he was not on duty up at Chorlbury Manor, but then he dismissed the idea. It would be rushing things. There would be other opportunities later.

He drove home whistling happily, and did not notice the tall figure of Mrs Fellowes waiting at the bus stop. Some way further on, however, he met a small girl standing by the roadside, thumbing a lift.

Major Johnson frowned. Small girls, and big ones too, should not thumb lifts from strangers. He slowed down. Only when the child was sitting beside him in the car and had said she wanted to go to Wiveldown did he realise who she was. Her name was Mary Forman, and her father worked in the paint factory where Major Johnson had been employed himself. Her mother had a job in a shop in Fleckington.

'You shouldn't be hitch-hiking, Mary,' Major Johnson reproved her. 'Isn't the bus due soon?'

'Yes. I'm meant to be on it,' Mary said. 'But lots of people from Wiveldown go to market and I knew I'd get a lift today. Then I can save the fare.'

'I hope you wouldn't go in a car with anyone you didn't know,' said Major Johnson.

She did not answer, busy picking at a sticking plaster on her knee.

'Will anyone be at home? Aren't your parents both at work?' He realised that she was adrift on a weekday because the schools were on holiday.

'I'm going to see my gran. She lives in Wiveldown too,' said Mary.

'Show me where her house is, and I'll drop you,' said the major.

III

Roger Brewis and Tom West loafed along an alley-way between a row of stalls in Leckington's market. It was

13

mid-afternoon, and the hot, late summer air was heavy with the threat of thunder. Scraps of paper and withered vegetable leaves littered the ground; babies in prams, some of them fractious and whining, blocked the aisles while their mothers gossiped or examined the goods and their brothers and sisters scuffled about in the dust.

The two boys wore skin-tight jeans into which their thin hips and legs seemed to have been poured, and despite the heat, leather jackets. Roger's was adorned with various symbols; Tom's was undecorated. Both wore their hair to their shoulders; Roger's was straight and lank, Tom's a mass of corkscrew curls which stood out like a halo round his pale face. They had spent a couple of hours earlier in the day going round the pubs in the centre of the town and drinking a pint of beer in each, and they had eaten, between them, a single packet of crisps. As they lurched along, Roger eyed the young women with their children and made loud remarks about them. Tom listened to him vaguely, his mind almost a blank; he felt sleepy.

They were both out of work. Tom had worked at a local garage, on the pumps, hoping to become a mechanic one day. The garage had been closed under a road-widening scheme and the owner had moved away from the district to open up elsewhere with his compensation money. Tom, meanwhile, was drawing his unemployment benefit and enjoying a rest. Roger had never had a steady job since he left school; two weeks here and three there was as much as he could manage. He'd sold small goods in an electrical store until the manager caught him stealing the stock; then he'd done a stint with a builder which had set him up financially for a time. He'd tried a milk round, but the early rising didn't really suit him.

They passed a vegetable stall. The stallholder was busy serving a crowd of women who were clustered round picking up apples, inspecting cauliflowers, and feeling plums for ripeness. Roger adroitly filched a small bunch of bananas from the front of the display and slipped them into an inside pocket in his jacket. He sauntered on, and when some yards past the stall started to fall about with laughter. Tom followed, slightly aghast but admiring. When they were well out of range, Roger shared his spoils and they ambled on, eating the bananas.

'Your turn next,' Roger said. 'I fancy some shoes. Them boots with studs round. Let's nick a pair.'

'We can't. We'd get caught,' Tom protested.

Roger had stopped at a footwear stall. Boots and shoes, men's, women's and children's, were arranged on a long trestle under an awning. Baskets of job lots, plimsolls and sandals, stood in front of the stall.

'That pair there.' Roger pointed. Some bright tan boots with studs over the instep had caught his fancy. 'Them's my size, nines. I'll chat up dad here, while you nick them. Meet you in the gents.'

He advanced to the edge of the trestle and leaned against it. The stallholder was showing cut-price sandals to a woman hung about with little children; a persistent toddler kept delving into the display basket as if it were a bran tub and coming up with assorted trophies. Out of the corner of his eye the trader had noticed the two boys, and he watched warily in seconds snatched from attending to the woman as Roger picked up a pair of canvas shoes and began to examine them.

Tom, with a sinking heart, looked at the boots. If he didn't do it, Roger would think him chicken, and he'd be right. It was just a lark, really, he reasoned. The boots weren't all that dear; Roger could pay for them if they were caught, since he'd cleaned up well on the building site and could always get taken on there again, for all he didn't fancy the work.

Someone would be sure to see, if he took them. There were so many people about, busybody women, if the stallholder himself didn't catch him in the act. Still, he could run. By the time they'd called the fuzz he'd be away. He glanced round. All the shoppers were intent on fighting their way through the narrow spaces between the stalls or spotting the best buys; they weren't looking at him. But the boots were bulky; he couldn't hide them.

At the far end of the stall Roger had picked up a lightweight shoe of the kind a clerk might wear. He ran his hand along its sole and peered inside it at the lining.

'Be with you in a minute, lad,' said the stallholder, handing his woman customer yet another sandal. 'Not your style, that, hardly,' he added to Roger.

'Take your time, dad. I'm not pushed,' Roger said. He leaned more heavily against the counter and over went several opened boxes of shoes on to the ground, spilling their contents. With an exclamation, Roger dived after them. 'Sorry, dad – clumsy, that's my trouble,' he gabbled, picking them up with every appearance of wanting to restore order.

Tom had seized his chance. He grabbed the boots and darted down another aisle to the rear of the shoe stall. Then he strolled along, holding them openly, so that they looked like an innocent purchase. He idled on, pausing to look at other things that caught his eye, one ear cocked listening for sounds of pursuit, but all was well. At the end of the gangway he put on speed and turned towards the public lavatories in a corner of the square. He pattered quickly down the steps and bolted himself into a cubicle until Roger should arrive. He felt slightly sick, yet elated. Beyond the odd apple or banana or a packet of sweets, he'd never stolen anything before.

IV

Mary Forman spent an hour with her grandmother in her council bungalow at the end of Welbeck Crescent and then she went home. The house, which was at the other end of the estate, was empty, since her parents were both still at work. She took the key from beneath a brick in the coal shed, unlocked the back door and let herself in, as she did after school every day. The house was very neat; it was well furnished, and in the kitchen there was a big refrigerator and a washing machine. A set of children's encyclopaedias on which Mary's mother was still paying the instalments filled a shelf in the living-room and there was an upright piano, for Mary was having music lessons. Mrs Forman was ambitious for her only child.

Mary sat at the piano and practised her scales a few times. Then she played two pieces she was learning. That would do for today. After that she went into the kitchen, poured herself out a glass of milk, opened a tin and took out three angel cakes, and then sat at the table to eat her small feast. She cleared up tidily after she had finished, for her mother had trained her to be neat. Then she went upstairs to change into her Brownie uniform. She and her friend Heather Smith were going to be tested for their Brownies' Writers' Badges at five o'clock.

The plaster on her knee needed replacing. A smear of blood had trickled down her leg from underneath it; all her picking at it must have re-opened the small wound. She went to the bathroom where the plasters were kept and carried out this repair. Then she fetched her school satchel, which contained her work to be examined, went downstairs, let herself out of the house, locked the door and put the key back in the coal shed.

Heather lived in a bungalow not far away. Wiveldown had been subjected to a good deal of in-filling development, and there was a close of eight new bungalows at the end of Church Street, one of which belonged to the Smiths. The arrangement was that Mary would call for Heather and they would walk together across the village to the cottage where Miss Evadne Price, who was to test them, lived. She was a retired school-mistress who now wrote historical romances and was thus doubly equipped for the job.

Heather's mother came to the door at Mary's ring, full of concern because Heather had been sick that afternoon and was not fit to go.

'Never mind. I'll go by myself,' said Mary.

'It's something she ate, I think – or this hot weather,' said Mrs Smith. She wondered for a moment if Mary ought to go alone and then dismissed her doubts. Miss Price lived in the village after all, and Mary was so sensible; she was used, too, to being on her own. There she stood, neat as a new pin, her

17

round pink face shining with health, the embodiment of the perfect Brownie.

'I tried to ring up Mrs Jenkins, but there was no answer,' Mrs Smith worried on. Mrs Jenkins was the Brown Owl who ran the Brownie pack and had made the appointment for the children with Miss Price. Twice Mrs Smith had been up to the call-box in the square trying to reach her.

'She's away. She's gone to Spain for a holiday,' said Mary. 'I hope Heather will be better soon,' she added. 'Now I'd better go.'

She walked off. The road wound round past the church, and she trod in sober fashion for in her Brownie uniform she felt old and important. She passed Major Johnson's bungalow; it looked deserted and the garage was closed but she heard a strange sound as she went by: the major was playing his trombone and the deep notes echoed into the outside world though all the windows were shut. Mary marched on. She jumped when a sudden rustling and then furious barking came from behind a privet hedge outside another house; a collie dog leaped at the gate, clawing the ironwork and making a frantic noise. Mary's heart thumped with fright as she hurried by, and a stern voice called the dog to order.

Soon she reached the square, where the road forked left for Fleckington and right for Chorlbury and the north. There was some traffic here. Her mother would be on the bus which arrived just before six but her father would be late, for on Thursdays in the summer he went straight from the factory to a house where he did odd-job gardening twice a week, and then on to a meeting of the Fleckington Caged Birds' Society. The Formans, between them, brought in a fair income, but their outgoings were heavy with their various hire-purchase commitments.

Duckett's Stores in the square closed on market days, but the post office was open. Mary had the money saved from her bus fare earlier, so she went in and bought some sweets. She did not like the two Mrs Flints, who were both sisters and sisters-in-law, having married a pair of brothers, but the post office was a useful place since it sold sweets as well as stamps, and also supplied the newspapers. The lino on the floor was always dirty, and the air seemed fusty. Mary did not know why she disliked the two Mrs Flints; they both wore crumpled clothes which looked as if they slept in them, and the ancient spaniel they owned had usually shed hairs upon them. Marilyn Flint was alone today since her sister was still at market; she looked stale, somehow, thought Mary, wrinkling her nose fastidiously as she went out again into the cleaner air of the square.

She put the sweets into her satchel to eat later. Beyond the square the road looped and a footpath between some buildings offered a short cut to the Leckington road where Miss Price lived. Mary took it, passing between two iron posts which were there to prevent bicycles being ridden this way. There were some tall white daisies growing in the rough grass at the side of the path, and Mary thought a bunch of them would make a nice present for Miss Price. As she moved about picking them, something caught her attention, an object lying in the grass; it was a shabby leather purse.

She picked it up. You took purses to the police, she knew, but there wasn't a policeman in the village now. Still, Dad or Mum would take it in to Leckington in the morning. She put it in her satchel.

V

After dropping Mary outside her grandmother's door, Major Johnson drove home, put his car away, and pottered round the garden snipping the odd dead head off the roses. There was not a weed to be seen; he had mowed the day before and the lawn was striped in neat swaths from the marks of the blades as though it had been swept. The air was heavy with the ominous stillness that precedes thunder and the sun was hidden now behind livid clouds. Soon he went indoors and took out the accounts of the Wiveldown Horticultural Society, of which he was the treasurer. He had taken on this task willingly, for he had plenty of spare time and he hoped it might be a way of being drawn into the life of the community. But he still felt a stranger, even though he was on nodding terms with many people. He did not play bridge, so he was excluded from the group who did, which included the Philpots next door. He went to church regularly, not from religious conviction but from habit begun when he joined the army as a band boy after his mother and father were killed in a railway accident. His only relative was an uncle who was a sergeant in a county regiment; it seemed the best solution at the time and he never questioned it, soon learning to play the bugle, and later the trombone. When the war came he transferred to the quarter-master's department where his meticulous sense of order had an outlet. He was quartermaster sergeant at the end of the war, and, remaining in the service, was commissioned soon afterwards.

Wiveldown's vicar was one of the bridge players. He was a scholarly widower round whom the ladies of the parish fluttered like solicitous doves. He was tall and looked distinguished, with white hair and a beaked nose; he should have been a bishop, thought Major Johnson, conscious every Sunday of his own small size beside the other man. The vicar had marked him down as someone likely to be useful, and with ready goodwill Major Johnson had run the tombola at the village fête and helped to trim the hedges round the churchyard, but he would not be drawn into the choir nor become a sidesman.

It was strange, he thought as he put away the accounts, now satisfactorily balanced, how you could live in a place for months and know many people by name, yet get close to no one. Still, it had always been like that for him, though he had never before had time to notice it. He looked around his sitting-room with its two armchairs upholstered in speckled hairy tweed; something was lacking here, but he did not know what it could be. Perhaps it was simply company.

Over the mantelpiece hung his bugle, which he polished twice every week. He kept his trombone in its case in his bedroom, and sometimes he got it out to play a few bars, when he thought there was no one near enough to hear him. Mrs Philpot was out a lot, at golf or bridge, and most afternoons Cathy Blunt from the other side, whose garden ran at right angles to his, went out with her new baby for a walk. Major Johnson intended to ask Miss Mainwaring if a trombone would be useful in Fleckington's amateur orchestra. He knew she played in it for he had seen her violin case in the library, and asked her. His wind was not as good as it had been, but he could still blow, and he had been commended often for his sense of timing.

He played a small part of a Gilbert and Sullivan overture, which had been a popular piece in his regiment's repertoire all those years ago; the notes scored for the trombone were not the most melodious, and to Mary Forman passing by, the sounds were like the braying of a donkey; but Major Johnson imagined himself back on the parade ground, stepping out with a light heart amid his fellow musicians.

He did not play for long. He wiped his mouth, his lips smarting a little because he played so seldom, and put the instrument away. He would have a bath and then go up to The Grapes. There were two pubs in the village, The Grapes and The Rising Sun, and Major Johnson had tried them both. The Grapes, besides being nearer, had a slightly older and less trendy clientele than The Rising Sun. He walked up there most evenings for a pint, and sometimes there was someone willing to chat in the bar.

As he soaped himself in the bath he heard a distant rumble of thunder, and when he opened the front door half an hour later the first huge drops of rain had begun to fall. Should he go? He would get soaked. Yet the evening would be long if he stayed at home. He had a television set, but he really only liked the football; plays and documentaries did not appeal to him and he seldom saw humour in the comedy shows. Mostly he read in the evenings.

He would get the car out and drive to The Grapes, even though it was only a few hundred yards away.

He backed it out, turned, and drove off through what was suddenly a deluge. Great gobbets of rain bounced up from the tarmac and thudded on the bonnet; already the gutters were full as torrents of water raced towards the drains. As he neared the pub he saw a figure scurrying along the road. It was a tall woman in a light jacket with a scarf tied over her head. She rushed into the pub ahead of him and stood gasping in the lobby. It was Mrs Fellowes.

'What a storm, Mrs Fellowes,' he exclaimed, following her inside.

'Oh – Major Johnson – yes – isn't it awful? I just came in here for shelter, I'm afraid.'

'You're soaked through,' he said, peering up at her. She had taken off her scarf and her grey hair hung damply round her face. 'Come along in and let me get you a drink.'

'Oh – you're very kind. Thank you,' she said.

He helped her off with her wet jacket and they went through into the bar. Nobody else was there; the evening was so bad that none of the regulars had turned out. A young girl with long, dark hair, wearing a purple dress that reached to her ankles, appeared from a side door and slipped behind the bar to serve them.

'Oh – Mrs Fellowes, it's you!' she said, sounding surprised.

'Hullo, Penny. So you're home. I thought you were off to Greece or somewhere,' said Mrs Fellowes.

'I go on Saturday – camping,' said the girl. She had a pale face and huge dark eyes. Major Johnson thought she looked half starved.

'This is Penny Hurst,' Mrs Fellowes told him. 'Major Johnson lives in the bungalow where the Boyds used to live, Penny. I don't think you've met, have you?'

They hadn't, but Major Johnson knew that the Hursts, who ran The Grapes, had a daughter at university.

'What can I get you?' Penny asked, leaning on the counter. Her hair fell forward, meeting under her chin. It must be a hazard when she pulled the beer, Major Johnson thought, imagining it dangling in the tankards. He persuaded Mrs

22

Fellowes to accept a whisky, since she'd got so wet, and had the same himself. Penny served them and then left, bidding them shout when they were ready for another. Mrs Fellowes smiled at her retreating back but Major Johnson was nonplussed at this abrupt treatment.

'She's packing, I expect,' said Mrs Fellowes. 'Though I suppose she'll only take a toothbrush and a bikini.'

'I'm not very used to young people, I'm afraid,' said the major, although it wasn't strictly true. He was accustomed to young men, but he soon disciplined them if they needed it. The girl had looked grubby, as well as famished, and there was no excuse for grime.

'She's a clever child,' said Mrs Fellowes. 'She's reading physics.'

'She looks as if she could do with a good meal,' said Major Johnson.

'That hungry look seems fashionable just now.' Mrs Fellowes sipped her drink. 'This is good,' she said. 'I don't come in here very often. That's why Penny looked surprised to see me. I've just had tea with Cathy Blunt, your neighbour.' Cathy had told her about presents of runner beans and lettuces offered over the hedge by the major.

Major Johnson knew the Blunts only slightly. The large, fair young man worked in insurance in Fleckington, and the new baby's reedy wail was a fresh sound in the neighbourhood. He rather liked hearing it; it was company, of a sort.

'You must let me drive you home,' he said. 'It's still raining hard. But have another drink first. Do you think your young friend will come if we call?'

'It would be kind of you to drive me,' Mrs Fellowes said. 'I was stupid to come out without a raincoat – at least I had a jacket. But you must have the second drink with me. I've got some whisky at home. Shall we go?'

The thought of summoning Penny Hurst from the inner fastness of the pub did not fill Major Johnson with enthusiasm.

'Very well,' he agreed.

Mrs Fellowes had finished her drink. She stood up.

23

While they were seated, Major Johnson had forgotten how tall she was, but now she loomed above him. She must weigh twelve stone, he thought. She was like a rather pleasant female sergeant-major, with her bright, intelligent eyes behind her glasses, and her fresh, healthy complexion.

He held her jacket while she slid her arms into it, and, standing on his toes, managed to hoist it part of the way up towards her shoulders. She shrugged it on, used to this difficulty.

She took up a great deal of room in the front of his car, and her grey flannel skirt billowed over the hand brake. Major Johnson felt quite awkward groping for it.

'Sorry,' she said, drawing back, quite unperturbed.

Her house was in Lammas Lane on the edge of the village; the lane wound round past it into open country and there were no other buildings near it. It was thatched, set back from the road up a bank, with a wooden fence and wicket gate, and a tall yew hedge behind the fence.

'We'll have to run for it,' said Mrs Fellowes as Major Johnson stopped the car, pulling it in as close to the side as he could. She hurried ahead of him, and had opened the front door by the time he got there. The rain was still spilling down, and a distant clap of thunder echoed. Major Johnson sped up the path past bent and dripping hollyhocks and entered the cottage.

VI

Roger put the stolen boots on in the lavatory, much to Tom's relief, and ditched his shabby canvas shoes. Next, he combed his lank hair and preened himself in the spotted mirror. Tom's curly mop was too tangled to submit to combing; he left it alone and leaned against the wall, waiting until Roger was satisfied with his own appearance. Then they emerged into the outer world.

Roger headed away from the market towards the shops, and Tom loped along beside him. They went through the swing doors of the big supermarket, where Roger picked up a wire basket. He walked slowly round posturing in front of the shelves and saying in a falsetto voice, 'Oh my, what have we here? Savoury snacks for dad's tea – how tempting,' and licking his lips. Tom was embarrassed by this exhibition until he saw a few smiles on the faces of ordinary shoppers. Roger put two small pork pies in his basket as they went round.

There was an off-licence in the store. Here, Roger once again surveyed the shelves. There was the usual range of wine, varying from bulk-bought plonk to a few vintage bottles, and a full complement of spirits. A number of customers were studying the display pensively, like readers in a library. Roger put a bottle of cheap red wine into his basket and then, with a movement which even Tom, who was agonisedly waiting for it, almost missed, slid a bottle of sherry into the big inside pocket of his jacket. Taking his time, he wandered on and added a swiss roll to what was in his basket. Then he gave the basket to Tom to take through the check-out and strolled on ahead of him, waiting among the discarded trolleys beyond the tills and whistling under his breath.

Tom had just enough money to pay for what was in the basket. He could have done without the wine and with bigger pork pies.

'What did you want to do that for?' he remonstrated when they were well away from the shop.

'Got it for my old gran, didn't I?' said Roger with a wink. 'It's easy. Them things is just asking to get nicked. It was whisky I was after, but there were two old bags standing in the way.'

'What're we going to do now, then?' Tom asked. He wanted to go home, but his mother would only look at him reproachfully and ask what he'd done about getting another job, and when his father got in he would lecture him too. And the house was so small. His two sisters would soon be back from work filling the place with their giggles and chatter.

'Going to have a bit of nosh,' said Roger. He was striding along, fast for him, since his usual speed was a fatigued amble.

They walked past the end of the market and down an alley where some of the stallholders parked their trucks. A few pick-ups and a number of lorries were drawn up by the kerb. There was no one about.

'Come on. Let's nip up here,' said Roger, and he shinned over the tailboard of a truck that had a canvas flap at the rear.

Tom followed. At least they were hidden from view inside the truck. It smelt of vegetables. There were some empty sacks on the floor.

'Make yourself comfortable. We've got a right palace here,' said Roger, doubling some sacks up under his thin buttocks. He produced a large knife from his pocket. It had a corkscrew among its numerous fitments and to Tom's eyes looked suspiciously new. More loot, he supposed. But with it, Roger dealt efficiently with the cork from the wine. He swallowed several mouthfuls and then passed the bottle to Tom. 'Here,' he said, 'have a bit.'

They stayed in the truck eating the pork pies and the swiss roll, and drinking the wine. Tom felt better after the food and some of his earlier sense of elation returned.

'Time to go,' said Roger, with one of his snap decisions. 'We'll find a couple of birds now.'

The shops and offices would soon be closing, and there would be girls in the streets, hurrying home or waiting for buses. It was a good idea. Flushed with wine, Tom quite fancied a bird. But they'd left it too late. Voices echoed from outside the truck. A sack of something was tossed through the canvas curtain. It smelt as if it was full of rotted cabbage stalks, and it landed almost on top of the boys as they retreated towards the driver's cab. Roger gripped Tom's arm. The truck rocked as someone got into the driver's seat and they heard the engine start. With several jerks the truck moved off.

The boys could have climbed out before it gathered speed, but they were taken by surprise and did not think fast enough. Before long they were travelling through the middle of the town.

Roger began to shake with suppressed mirth.

'What a giggle,' he whispered. 'Wonder where we're going?'

In fact they drove for ten miles. Then the truck bumped over a rough track and finally stopped. The engine was switched off and the driver got out. Now they'd be caught. Tom told himself that they would be found guilty only of a minor offence, a prank, and if the man was decent he might let them off without calling the police. He wouldn't know about the stolen sherry or the boots. His heart thudded painfully against his ribs as he waited for discovery.

But there was total silence. No one came to the back of the truck. After a time they looked out. The truck was parked in a large barn among bales of hay stacked up to the rafters. The doors stood open, and outside rain was spilling down from the sky as though some giant waterfall was dropping from the heavens.

VII

Miss Price's cottage had very small lattice windows peering out at the world from under its thick thatch, and inside it was very dark. Mary had never been there before. Miss Price was old, but she rode about the village and for miles around on an ancient, upright bicycle, wearing in winter a flowing black cloak. The younger children thought she was a witch, but she had no cat, only a budgerigar which warbled now from its cage in a corner of the living-room. Mary looked round with interest. The walls and ceiling were criss-crossed with beams, and the room was full of heavy old furniture. At one end of it was a loom, for Miss Price wove her own tweed and had made the fabric of the sweeping full skirt she wore now in the manner of one of her heroines. The table at which she wrote her books, in longhand using plain pen and ink, stood in the middle of the room. Two reference books were open on it, and a pile of manuscript covered in neat writing was stacked under a piece of pink blotting paper with a model of Edinburgh Castle on top of it acting as a paper-weight.

It was all most unlike Mary's house in Welbeck Crescent, and Miss Price was not at all like either Mary's mother or her grandmother.

'I taught your mother at Leckington Secondary Modern School not so long after the war,' Miss Price remembered. 'Is she still working in the ironmonger's?'

'No. She's at Moffat's now, in the millinery department,' Mary said.

'Hm. Able girl. Should have got herself some training,' grunted Miss Price. 'Selling hats, is she? No one wears them now, do they?'

'She does the knitwear too,' Mary offered. Miss Price was rather alarming. She wore her white hair in a plait pinned round her head, and her eyes were dark and seemed to see right through you.

'Knitwear, indeed. Jumpers and cardigans, Mary. Jumpers and cardigans. All these euphemisms – terrible. Millinery and knitwear – it's disgraceful. Say what you mean, my dear, in clear language, and you won't go wrong. Now, what have you got to show me?'

Timidly, Mary produced the poem and the story she had written. Part of the test had to be conducted under the examiner's eye, and while Miss Price read these efforts, putting on a pair of steel-rimmed glasses to do so, she wrote a letter to an imaginary aunt. When all this was done Miss Price, who had mellowed while she looked at Mary's work, pointed out some spelling errors and a split infinitive. There was no serious fault to be found, however, and the Brownie badge was safely won. Miss Price wrote out the certificate which Brown Owl would present at the next meeting. Then she gave Mary a glass of milk and a piece of sponge cake, and showed her how the loom worked. Mary was allowed to weave several rows of the black and yellow fabric that was threaded up. She was fascinated by how the various strands were raised and lowered by the treadles. Because of her interest, Miss Price said she would invite all the Brownies up another day to see it, and Mary left.

She walked down the road, still feeling important in her

uniform, but lighthearted now, secure in her achievement. When she had gone a little way she opened her satchel to get out the sweets. There was the purse. It was quite bulgy. Whoever it belonged to must be worried if it was full of money.

She opened it. There were a great many coins – about two pounds – and a few notes tucked into the flap. There was also a pension book. Mary took it out and read the name. It belonged to Mrs Ellen Pollock, of *The Hollies*, Wiveldown. That was old Mrs Pollock who lived in the last house in the village along the Leckington road. She lived alone with her cat, and her garden was a wild jungle. The village children told frightened tales about her; she was sometimes seen shuffling along, bent almost double, on her way to the post office. Mary had once opened the door for her and been thanked in a high, clear voice and rewarded with a smile of extraordinary sweetness and a mild glance from faded blue eyes.

Mary was not afraid of her, even if she was a hermit. She would take the purse back to her. It wouldn't take long.

She turned about and set off, hopping along now, her fair hair flopping on her shoulders. She did not notice how black the sky had grown, but the first rumble of thunder sounded as she opened Mrs Pollock's gate. The drive was full of grass and creeping weed. Tall shrubs loomed on either side, and the scent of old-fashioned roses filled the air with a heavy fragrance. Mary sniffed it as she walked along.

The rain began as she reached the front door. It was painted black, and the paint was peeling from it. The knocker was too high for Mary to reach. She flapped the letter box, but it did not make much noise. Then she noticed a knob beside the door; it was an old-fashioned bell-pull, something Mary had never seen before, but she caught hold of it and tugged, and immediately a jangle echoed from within the house. After a long time she heard scuffling sounds from the other side.

'Who's there?' called a voice.

'I'm Mary Forman. I've found your purse,' piped Mary. Raindrops were plopping now on her head and making marks as big as pennies on the step she stood on.

She heard the rasp of a bolt being drawn and the door of the house opened a little way. Two blue eyes, not mild now, but wary, regarded her. The little old lady was not much taller than Mary was herself. She was very wrinkled, and she smelt rather, a bit like the ladies in the post office yet differently. She was not at all alarming.

'Mary Forman, eh? So that's your name. I remember you,' said Mrs Pollock.

'Your purse,' said Mary, holding it out. 'It is yours, isn't it? I found it on the path by the square.'

'That's mine all right. Come along in, child,' said Mrs Pollock, opening the door wider.

Mary had not meant to go into the house, but it was raining now in earnest and there was a sudden louder clap of thunder while she hesitated. It made her jump, and she skipped across the threshold. Mrs Pollock laughed. At least, Mary supposed that the cackling sound was laughter.

'Don't like thunder, do you? Well, never mind. It'll pass. I'll be glad of company while the storm lasts,' said the old woman.

'I opened your purse to see whose it was,' said Mary. She handed it to Mrs Pollock. 'I saw your pension book. I didn't touch anything except to read the address on the book.'

'What a good thing you found it, a nice little girl like you and not some good-for-nothing lout,' said Mrs Pollock. 'Though I don't suppose all those long-haired lads are wicked either,' she added in a mumble to herself. She looked inside the purse. 'Everything's there. You're a good girl.' She took out a fifty-pence piece. 'You shall have this as a reward.'

'Oh no,' protested Mary. 'Please keep it.'

She tried to press the coin back into Mrs Pollock's skinny hand. The old lady was obviously very poor and couldn't spare it. Her clothes were dirty and ragged and the house was in a shocking state. The lino in the hall where they were standing was worn into holes and the wallpaper was faded and stained. All the furniture was smothered in dust.

'You take it,' Mrs Pollock said. She popped it into a pocket of Mary's dress and patted her. 'Now, come along into the kitchen. We'll be warm there. You can't go home till the storm is over.'

She put the purse into a drawer in the heavy carved sideboard in the hall and hobbled off towards the back of the house. Mary followed. They went through a door and along a flagged passage into the kitchen. This was a much nicer part of the house. There was a Rayburn stove in front of which slept the tabby cat. Red and white checked curtains, rather grubby but still bright, hung at the windows, and there was a big deal table. Two dilapidated wicker chairs with patchwork cushions stood on either side of the range. Mary wondered how such a bent old lady managed to fill it; she knew that no one came to the house to help her. She had lived like a recluse for years and would let no one in, not even the vicar or the meals-on-wheels ladies. Mr Duckett, from the stores, who ran a delivery service, dropped her a regular order once a week; she left a box for it on the step, and the money for the previous week's purchase, but she never spoke to him.

'Let's have a cup of tea,' said Mrs Pollock.

Mary was still full of the milk and cake she had had with Miss Price, but it would have been rude to refuse.

'I'll make it,' she said, and bustled about doing so while her hostess sat back in her wicker chair, knobbled hands plucking at her skirt, directing operations in her oddly high voice. Outside the storm grew loud and frightening, but the two sat snug. Mrs Pollock wanted to know all about the Brownies, and what Mary thought of school. It seemed that she remembered Mary's father from when he was a boy; he had always lived in the village, but she did not know Mary's mother. They had a most interesting talk, and Mrs Pollock told Mary what things had been like when she was a girl. She remembered quite clearly the day that Queen Victoria had died. All this passed the time most agreeably while the thunder rumbled overhead and the rain poured down. It streamed against the windows and rushed out of the gutters in great jets.

'This is a solid house,' said Mrs Pollock. 'Men knew how to

31

build in those days – not like the dolls' houses they build now.'

Mary supposed the old lady would think her home a doll's house. It certainly was tiny compared with Mrs Pollock's, but she preferred it. This house was gloomy; it smelt damp; and all the furniture was huge and ugly. Mrs Pollock took her into the room she called the parlour and showed her faded photographs of Mr Pollock in his soldier's uniform. He wasn't really old enough to fight in the Boer War, Mary learned, but he had lied about his age and been accepted. Mary had never heard of the Boer War till now. He and Mrs Pollock had come to live in this house fifty years ago. Mary wasn't quite sure how long Mr Pollock had been dead, but it was obviously a very long time, and the pictures of Mrs Pollock's son and his wife showed what looked to Mary an old man and woman. They lived in Australia and had a sheep farm, and four sons, all married with still more children. It was rather confusing, and Mrs Pollock herself seemed muddled about who was who. They'd wanted her to go out to Australia to live with them, but she'd refused.

'I'm too old to move,' she said. 'I manage.'

They went back to the kitchen and Mrs Pollock settled down in her chair again while Mary washed up the tea things. It was still raining, but the thunder had faded into the distance. When she had put away the cups and saucers and the chipped brown teapot Mary saw that Mrs Pollock had fallen asleep. She sat there, her head resting on the back of the chair, wispy grey hair framing her wrinkled face, her mouth a little open, breathing heavily.

Mary felt she ought to go. Her parents might wonder where she was – well, her mother might. Dad wouldn't be home. She had no idea of the time and there wasn't a clock to be seen. But it would be rude to go without saying goodbye, and it was still raining quite hard. Probably her mother would think she had stayed with Miss Price till the storm ended. What a funny day she had had, visiting these two old ladies in their two different sorts of houses. She did not realise that Mrs Pollock was almost twenty years older than Miss Price.

There was a row of books on the dresser. Mary went over to

look at them. One was *David Copperfield*. She took it down and began to read it. It was a long book and the print was small, but she skipped the first part and soon found it absorbing in an odd, slow way. There were pictures in it, too. It was only gradually that she realised there was something wrong in the room. She lifted her head. Mrs Pollock's breathing had stopped and there was silence.

The old woman looked just the same. Her mouth was still open and her hands were still folded on her lap.

'Mrs Pollock!' Mary said in a shaky voice, and then again more loudly, 'Mrs Pollock!'

The cat stirred. It got to its feet slowly, then stretched and crossed to its mistress. It pawed at her skirt and then mewed. The plaintive sound was eerie in the still room. Mary's heart began to race. She approached the old lady. 'Mrs Pollock?' she said again. There was no answer.

She's ill, thought Mary.

She must get the doctor. She was a capable child, and though she was frightened she did not panic immediately. There was a rug on an upright chair in a corner of the room, and she picked it up to cover the old lady's knees so that she would catch no chill while Mary went for help. As she tried to tuck it round the skinny form, Mrs Pollock's hands fell from her lap and swung limply at her sides. Her head sagged against the chair and her mouth fell further open.

Mary did not wait. She ran to the hall, wrenched open the door and raced down the drive as fast as her terrified legs would carry her.

Behind her the door of the house swung to again and shut.

VIII

While the storm was raging overhead, Roger and Tom sheltered in the barn. They had no idea where they were, but it was warm and dry in their refuge. The climbed up the hay bales and found a hollow where they would be hidden from anyone entering the barn.

'We're right enough here,' Roger said. 'No hurry to get away.'

'How'll we know where we are?' Tom asked, but he did not really mind about that. They were safe from being caught in possession of stolen goods, and no one would ever know they had been in the truck. They could easily creep out from here later on.

'We'll follow the track. It'll go to a road somewhere. Must do,' Roger said. 'Pity we never got them birds.'

Tom thought it was lucky. Girls would have giggled and squealed and they'd have been discovered.

Roger was opening the bottle of sherry.

'Come on. Have a swig,' he said.

They finished it before the storm was over. Roger had the lion's share, but Tom drank a great deal of it and his head felt very swimmy. He kept wanting to giggle and his legs felt weak. Roger seemed unaffected by all that he had drunk so Tom kept quiet about the effect it had on him. After a time the thunder faded away and the rain slacked off. Roger thought it was time to go.

They looked out of the barn door and saw that they were in a farm yard. Rain dripped from the eaves of every building and there were puddles on the ground. A tractor was parked against one wall, but there was no one in sight. Nervously at first, but then with increasing confidence, they passed the sheds and went under an arch that marked the end of the yard.

'We're in luck. The farmhouse must be up the other way,' said Roger. They stood under the arch looking at the track which stretched away ahead of them, its ridge still firm though twin rivers of water filled the ruts on either side. There was a door under the archway and Roger opened it. It revealed a shed which housed farming implements – there were a harrow and some rakes and a small trailer. There were also two bicycles, one gleaming new machine with upright handle-bars, chopper type, and a smaller ordinary one.

'Phew, what luck,' said Roger. He grabbed the taller bicycle and wheeled it out. 'It's O.K. No one's about,' he said, and pedalled off.

Tom would rather have chanced it on his feet, but he did not want to be left behind. He took the other one and followed. It was much too small for him, and his knees stuck out as he tried to keep them clear of the handle-bars. Roger was rapidly vanishing into the distance. The track ran through a field and ended in a gateway leading into a tarmac lane; Roger had turned to the left and Tom went after him. The going was easier on the hard surface of the lane. It was still raining, but not hard; thunder rumbled in the distance.

'This is great,' said Roger, leaning back, hands high in front of him.

'Great,' echoed Tom, saving a skid.

They rode for about three miles, meeting no one, and then their lane joined a bigger road. A finger post pointed back the way they had come. It said: *Mordwell Village Only*. Neither of them knew where Mordwell was.

'Must be a crummy place,' said Roger.

They pedalled on. A car came up behind them and blew its horn; Tom braked and wobbled into position behind Roger as it passed them, spattering up water and drenching their legs. Roger shook his fist as it disappeared.

After ten minutes more riding they could see a thirty-mile-an-hour traffic sign ahead.

'We're getting somewhere now,' said Roger. 'Must be houses there. We'd better ditch the bikes. We'll hitch a ride.'

Tom was thankful to fall in with this idea. They stopped at the next gateway. It was securely locked with a padlock and chain but they lifted the bicycles over it, wheeled them a little way into the field along the hedge and laid them down in the long grass at the side of it. It was a field used for grazing cattle, though it was now being rested, but the two town boys did not realise this. They were simply thankful to meet no cattle face to face.

Once they were back in the road again they walked on towards the traffic signs. Nothing passed them. This was not a much-used road. Their legs in the thin jeans were soaked but their thick jackets had kept their bodies dry. Roger's hair hung down in rat's tails round his head; Tom's curls stood out in a wild fuzz.

Near the thirty-limit sign was another which gave the village's name: *Wiveldown*.

'Ever been here before?' asked Roger.

'Yes,' said Tom. 'Came here with the football team.'

Before he met Roger he had played for Leckington Colts.

'I haven't. Dead and alive, isn't it?'

Tom had thought it rather a pretty, peaceful little place but he said nothing. They walked on. The rain had come on harder again and they hunched their shoulders against it. They passed a few cottages which showed no sign of life and then they came to a fork in the road. Neither knew which way to turn for Leckington, and there was no signpost, so Roger tossed a coin and they took the left fork.

'What a deserted place,' said Tom as they plodded on. He remembered a village square, a church, at least one pub and some shops. He'd certainly never been down these by-ways. His head no longer felt swimmy, but he had a remote feeling, as though all this was happening to someone else.

They did not notice the car until they were almost upon it. It was drawn well into the side of the road on the grass verge, bonnet towards them.

'Wonder if it's locked,' said Roger. 'We might sit in the dry for a bit.'

'I can open it, even if it is,' boasted Tom. 'I've got a bit of wire.' He had not worked in a garage for nothing.

'Right, then. Let's try it,' said Roger.

But they did not have to force it; it wasn't locked.

They sat inside, their breath steaming up the windows, while the rain fell steadily.

'Could you drive this crate?' Roger asked after a while.

'Course I could,' said Tom. 'I can drive anything.'

'There isn't no key. Could you start it?'

'Course,' said Tom again.

'Well, get on with it, then. We'll drive it home and leave it in the car park.'

'Oh no!' Tom said, but then the idea began to appeal to him. The bloke shouldn't have left it like this, just asking to be nicked. And he was sick of being second fiddle to Roger. Here was something he could do and Roger couldn't.

He pulled a lock under the dash to open the bonnet, then got out into the teeming rain, raised the lid and fiddled with the engine. Roger looked impressed when soon it was running. Tom adjusted the choke with an important air. When he'd said that he could drive he'd been exaggerating. Sometimes while minding the pumps he'd moved the occasional car around the forecourt, but he'd never been on the open road. However, he found first gear and with only a few jerks crawled off down the lane.

'We've got to turn,' he said.

He drove back to the junction where they had tossed for their route, managed to reverse into the other road, and swung round with some panache. As they moved forward again Roger leaned across and tooted the horn.

'What d'you want to do that for?' demanded Tom. Like many another man behind the wheel of a car, he now felt a great sense of power. He speeded up and changed gear. The wipers, which had been left on and so worked automatically when the engine was started, scraped back and forth distractingly in front of him and the rain fell down in blinding sheets. He turned his head to look at Roger.

'Look out – ' Roger cried, leaning forward.

Tom barely heard him. He was only half aware of a blur in front of him before there was a heavy thud. The car went on, thumping over something.

'For Christ's sake stop!' screamed Roger.

At last Tom found the brake and stopped the car. Roger was out in a flash but Tom could not move at first. Then his limbs unfroze and he followed. Roger had run back the way they had come, and Tom found him standing over the body of a little girl lying in the road. One hand was turned palm upwards to

37

the sky, and as they watched the fingers slowly uncurled and then were still.

'You ran right over her,' Roger said.

'I never saw her,' Tom whimpered. He began to tremble. 'A doctor! We must get a doctor!'

Roger looked down at the child.

'Ain't you never seen a dead rabbit?' he asked. 'A doctor won't help this kid.'

'Oh no!' wailed Tom. 'I never saw her,' he said again. 'Where'd she come from?'

'Must have been walking in the road,' said Roger.

'It wasn't my fault,' Tom cried and began to sob.

Roger slapped him sharply across the face.

'Maybe not, but no one's going to believe you,' he said. 'We've got to get out of here. Cut out that snivelling.' He walked back to the car and tried the boot. It was unlocked. Roger returned to the child, picked up her limp body and carried it back to the car, where he laid it, none too gently, in the boot, beside a petrol tin and a bag of tools. He closed the lid.

'Now, get that car turned round and put it back where you found it,' he said. 'Quick, before someone comes along.'

Still sobbing, Tom climbed back into the car. Somehow he managed to start it. He went up the road and found a place to turn. When he came back, grinding along in first gear, Roger had disappeared.

PART TWO

I

ON FRIDAY morning the air was fresh and sweet after the storm, and the sky was streaked with clouds which gradually dispersed as the sun rose. The day began for most people in Wiveldown in the normal way. Two milkmen made rounds in the village, one at half-past six and his rival at ten. Major Johnson patronised the early one; he seldom slept later than six, so he got up then and made tea, which he drank in his dressing-gown before he washed and shaved. He was always astir before anyone else in the road. Soon after seven a few cars would pass, driven by men on their way to various factories, and later a tractor might clatter by. The newspapers were unreliable at the moment because of the school holidays; in term-time they were delivered by a boy before the school day began.

Major Johnson could set his watch by the timetables of his neighbours. Derek Blunt left for his insurance office in Leckington at a quarter to nine. A new part of routine was Cathy Blunt's morning trip down her garden soon after nine to put out her washing; a row of white nappies would flutter like bunting from her line, visible to Major Johnson from his patio.

On the other side of the major lived the Philpots. The land where his house and the Blunts' were had originally been theirs, but they had sold it for development. Mr Philpot was a butcher; he owned more land on the far side of the village and kept cattle and sheep there before they were slaughtered. Cathy was glad he did not fatten them where she could see them; she told Major Johnson when they were talking over the fence one day that she did not fancy buying chops from beasts she'd seen on the hoof.

39

Mr Philpot had a shop in Leckington and others in two large villages in the county; he was often in The Grapes in the evening when the major went there and was friendly over a pint, but he was usually in the midst of his friends while the major sat quietly in a corner taking small part in the conversation, for what did he know of beef and farming?

Mr Philpot left home at ten to nine most days, but earlier on market days. Mrs Philpot played golf and went off early on Tuesdays and Thursdays to the golf club. Friday was her day for shopping and she stayed in Leckington for lunch. She played bridge too, and in fact was seldom at home during the day. Major Johnson did not know if they had any children; they must be adult now, if so. Perhaps there were grandchildren, but he had not heard of any. Mrs Philpot with her bright chestnut hair didn't look very grandmotherly, but appearances were deceptive. Mrs Fellowes, now, was different. He could easily imagine her as a grandmother, with her grey hair and generous curves, but her only daughter, now working as a secretary in Vancouver, was not married. She had a son working in London in television; he was married but he had no children.

They'd had a very pleasant evening. Major Johnson had been able to admire from the window her garden, which was full of roses, michaelmas daisies and dahlias. She grew soft fruit to sell: raspberries and strawberries, and currants. In the end he'd stayed to supper. She'd produced delicious chilled watercress soup, left from some party she'd had the day before, and had made a fluffy omelette, filling it with chicken.

'What would you have had at home?' she'd asked him, as they ate this meal in her kitchen. She'd spread a checked cloth on the round table, and drawn the blinds to shut out the weather. They'd eaten by candlelight.

'Oh –' Major Johnson looked sheepish. 'Egg and bacon, probably.'

'Did the lessons help?'

'Oh yes. I can give a dinner party now,' said Major Johnson. But he hadn't yet. However, in the autumn he would do it. He would ask the Philpots, and, naturally, Miss Mainwaring. He might even include Mrs Fellowes and the vicar, if he felt bold enough to cope with six.

They talked about Chorlbury Manor, where Mrs Fellowes had been a guide for years. She knew Admiral Bruce, the curator, and his wife quite well. Mrs Bruce had started a garden centre which operated in the walled garden and was a great success.

'She's used to organising naval wives, she needed something to do,' said Mrs Fellowes.

'The admiral was lucky to find a job like that,' said Major Johnson. 'I wish I could do the same, but then I'm not an admiral. All I could find were clerking jobs.' He told her about his stint in the paint factory.

'What did you do in the army?' asked Mrs Fellowes.

He told her the whole story, from his enlistment in the band as a boy, covering the time at Tobruk where his contribution was not glorious, but necessary, and the months afterwards when he had been in charge of prisoners in Italy. After the war he had been to the Far East, and to Germany; he had finished his career in Aldershot. He hid no unglamorous facts from her; she heard it all.

'How well you've done. You must be proud,' she said.

He looked astonished.

'I've nothing to show for it. No medals. No high rank.'

'But you started as a boy – all alone. I think it's splendid,' said Mrs Fellowes warmly. 'And your trombone. Do you play it still?'

'Only if I'm sure the Philpots and the Blunts can't hear me. It would annoy them,' he said.

'You ought to join the orchestra,' she said, putting his ambition into words. 'Celia Mainwaring will know about it.'

So her name was Celia. He had not known what the C stood for, and had guessed Cynthia, Cecily, and Charlotte, but never Celia.

'She does so much,' said Mrs Fellowes. 'At Christmas the amateur dramatic society will be doing *The Mikado* – they do a

41

Gilbert and Sullivan every year, much better than a panto-mime. Sometimes Celia acts, and sometimes she plays in the orchestra. She's so good at both, she needs to be cut in two.'

Major Johnson was sure that this was so.

'Do you perform?' he asked.

'I help with costumes,' Mrs Fellowes said. 'It's difficult for me to get into the town at night – I've no car and the buses aren't good. And I can't act or sing. I'm much too big. I'd be well cast as Katisha if I'd got the voice.'

'I've never done any acting,' said Major Johnson, who was uncertain if he understood the allusion. Wasn't Katisha the woman who had a caricature of a face? 'It must be difficult, living out here without a car,' he added.

'My daughter thinks I should move to a town. London for choice. But I love this village. I've lived here for so long. And I love this cottage too.'

'Don't you drive at all?'

'Oh, heavens, yes. I ran a car until fairly recently. But it's such an expense, I sold it. Sometimes I hire one, for holidays. I keep my licence up. I bicycle a lot,' she said.

Major Johnson had seen her pedalling along, a bulky figure dressed in slacks.

'How do you get to Chorlbury?' he asked.

'Madge Fazackerley takes me.'

Another guide. He knew her by sight.

'She's a great friend of Olive Philpot's. They play golf and bridge together,' said Mrs Fellowes. 'Bill Fazackerley farms the land between here and Mordwell.'

Major Johnson knew nothing of who owned what beyond the limits of the village. Mrs Fellowes told him about the changes she had seen since she came to live in Wiveldown. The village was no longer, as she put it, truly rural; now it was becoming a dormitory for the nearby towns where industry was develop-ing.

Major Johnson did not leave until eleven o'clock, so swiftly fled the time, but it was of Miss Mainwaring that he thought as he composed himself for slumber, not his hostess of the evening.

42

When Mary had not come home by seven o'clock on Thursday evening, her mother did not worry. It was raining hard; Mary must be sheltering from the storm either at Miss Price's house, or with her friend Heather Smith. She often spent the evening with the Smiths. The storm lasted for a long time, and before it ended Mrs Forman had to go out herself to a meeting of the Wives' Club. She left some ham and salad ready for Mary's supper and a note telling her to go straight to bed. Joe would not be back till late from his Caged Birds' Society meeting, but Mary was used to being left. She was eleven now, and a sensible child.

It was after half-past ten when Mrs Forman got back to find Mary's supper untouched and her room empty. For a moment she could not take in what this meant; then she began to wonder frantically what had happened. The Smiths would never have kept her for the night without sending a message, but they would know what time the girls had returned from seeing Miss Price. She rushed round to their bungalow.

They had gone to bed. Ted Smith came to the door in his trousers with his shirt off.

'It's Jean Forman,' he called to his wife. 'Seen Mary?'

Betty Smith came into the hall wearing a flowered dressing-gown.

'Come in, Jean, do – it's still raining, isn't it?' she said. 'Isn't Mary home, then?'

'No. I thought she must be waiting with you till the storm finished. I've been at the Wives' Club. I thought you'd be there too.'

'No, I couldn't go. Our Heather's been sick. She couldn't go with Mary this afternoon.'

'Mary didn't come back here, then?'

'No, love. Oh – you mean she hasn't been home at all?'

Both women stared at each other.

'I did wonder if she ought to go alone – but Miss Price lives right in the village and it was daylight – she'd have been back in an hour or so. Perhaps she took shelter there. Ted'll pop up and see,' said Betty. 'You come along in, Jean.'

Ted had disappeared during this interlude and he returned now, wearing a sweater. He carried a torch.

'I heard. I'll go there right away, Jean. You stay here.'

'I'd best go home. She might come back,' said Mrs Forman. 'Isn't Joe there?'

'It's his night for the caged birds. He won't be back for a bit.' And then he'll be full of beer, Jean thought.

'You'd better go, then. But she'll be safe and sound at Miss Price's, you'll see. I expect she's staying there because of the storm.'

No one mentioned the fact that there had been a lull earlier.

'Miss Price would never have kept her without sending a message. She's on the phone.'

'Yes, but you aren't. And maybe the lines have been affected by the lightning,' said Ted, on a flash of inspiration. He was sure that something serious had happened, but Jean dissolving into hysterics would help no one. 'We'll soon find out. I'll get up there now, and I'll come straight round to your place after – with Mary, likely enough.' Mentally, he crossed his fingers.

The women watched while he put on his raincoat and his wellington boots and then started up the road. When his bulky presence had left them they felt curiously forlorn.

'I'll be going, then,' said Jean Forman bleakly.

'Yes, love. I'd come with you, but I can't leave Heather.'

'No – of course not. It'll be all right,' said Jean.

'Of course it will. What could happen to her here in Wiveldown, where she knows everybody, pretty nearly?' Betty Smith said stoutly.

Jean repeated this reassuring statement to herself as she walked home. She had left the lights on, but no one was there. Joe came in ten minutes later. She heard the car, but she did not go to meet him.

As she had expected, he smelt strongly of alcohol and took a minute or two to grasp what she told him when he came into the house.

'We must get the police,' she said. 'Go and telephone them, Joe.'

'We must wait till Ted gets back,' Joe said. 'He'll have found Mary up at Miss Price's, you'll see. I'll take the car and go up after him.'

'No, don't. You shouldn't be driving, you're full of beer.' Jean said. 'You'll make things worse. I'll put the kettle on. You need some coffee.'

She was white-faced with shock. Joe watched her mutely while she made two strong cups of instant coffee, and tried to pull his errant wits together while he drank his. They sat in silence, waiting for Ted.

Miss Price had gone to bed and was reading a book on spiritualism when she heard him banging at her door. She thought he was some malefactor, and took a good deal of persuading before she would open it, but at last he convinced her that he was in fact Ted Smith, foreman at Walter's, the paint factory in Leckington. She opened the door and was revealed to him in a man's woollen dressing-gown with her grey hair in a long plait over one shoulder. Her glasses were on and she still held her book, with a finger between the pages marking her place.

'What do you want at this time of night, young man?' she demanded.

'I'm looking for Mary Forman. She's missing from home. Did she come for her Brownie test today?'

'Of course she did. Right on time. And a very nice, polite child she is too,' said Miss Price. 'Did you say she never went home?'

Ted repeated the facts.

'She left here at six. No later,' said Miss Price. 'You'd better ring up the police. Come in. The phone's on the window here.'

'Her parents must do it. She may have turned up,' said Ted. 'You'll let me know at once if she's safe?'

'Certainly.'

45

Ted left her standing there framed in the lighted doorway, a bulky, imposing figure. She turned slowly back into the house and closed the door. Then she sat down in the chair beside the hearth to wait until the police came, for come they would, she knew. Presently the habit of a lifetime reasserted itself and she began to read again.

Ted hurried back towards the centre of the village. As he walked at top speed down Church Street towards the turning for Welbeck Crescent where the Formans lived, a car passed him. It was a dark car, black or some similar colour, a Morris or Austin 1300. It drove on, its tail-lights dwindling into the distance. Then he saw it turn to the right, somewhere near where Mr Philpot the butcher and his wife lived in their large, mock-Georgian house.

III

Two uniformed policemen in a Panda car arrived at the Formans' house six minutes after Joe's telephone call. They were brisk but kind, and their expressions were grave as they listened to Jean's account of Mary's movements, as far as they were known. One of them then went out to the car, and the other asked some more questions.

'Has she any other friends where she might have gone for the night?'

'She's plenty of friends, but she's never stayed away for the night except at the Smiths' or her granny's,' said Jean.

'Her granny? Where's that?'

Joe explained that his mother lived at the other end of the estate in a council bungalow.

'Mary'd never stay there without leaving a message,' he said.

'Maybe your mother sent someone down with a message and it didn't arrive – some other child, perhaps,' said the constable. 'We'll soon find out.'

At this possibility both Jean and Joe brightened. They supplied a list of the names of her friends, and explained about Mrs Jenkins, the Brown Owl, to whom ordinarily Mary might have gone after the test to report on her success.

'On holiday, is she? And Mary knew it?' The young policeman made a note.

'Had she anything on her to show who she was?' he asked. 'Her name on her clothes?'

'She'd her satchel with her. It's not in her room. She'd have her work in that for Miss Price to see. Why – ?'

'If she's not at her grandmother's, we'll be trying the hospitals in case there's been an accident, Mrs Forman,' he said.

The second policeman now returned.

'Chief Inspector Coward's on his way over,' he told the Formans. 'He'll be here directly. We'll be off now to follow up these addresses.'

The two constables went away. Joe accompanied them to their car, and when he came back his face was grim. He was completely sober now.

'We never should have left her on her own, a little girl like that,' he said.

'It's serious? The bobbies think it's bad?' Jean asked. Both of them knew now that Mary was not with her grandmother; it could not be so simple.

'They do. I told you it wasn't right to leave her,' Joe said. 'You should have stayed at home.' His mind was full of horrifying images of what might have happened to his child.

'Well, I'll be off,' said Ted, acutely embarrassed by this exchange. 'Don't want Betty starting to worry.'

'Oh – right, Ted. And thanks,' said Joe.

Jean took no notice as Ted left the room. Her eyes were fixed on Joe.

'You're glad enough to have the things my money buys,' she said. 'Besides, I want Mary to have a chance. I never had nice things when I was her age.'

'She'd be right enough on what I get,' said Joe. 'I bring a decent packet home, good enough for most. You could have

47

got a job here in Wiveldown, if you'd a mind, cleaning and that. They'd have let you take Mary along in the holidays.'

But Jean Forman was far above domestic work.

It was into this charged atmosphere that Detective Chief Inspector Coward and Detective Sergeant Davis arrived. The air between husband and wife was so tense that they felt it the moment they entered the house.

'Any news?' asked Joe.

'Not yet, Mr Forman,' said the chief inspector. He was a burly middle-aged man, and he had daughters of his own. 'There's no report of any road accident involving a child in this vicinity this evening, and she isn't in Leckington hospital. We're making enquiries further away. Would she accept a ride in a car with a stranger, do you think?'

'She's been told over and over not to,' said Jean.

'Some of these men can be very persuasive,' said the chief inspector. 'I'm sorry to alarm you, but we must bear in mind this possibility.'

'Of course,' said Joe. 'It's what I thought of straight away.'

The older man gave him a sympathetic look. A swift glance round the Formans' living-room had shown him a lot: a new three-piece suite, bought on the never-never for sure; a potted hydrangea; framed prints on the wall which were the same as a series his wife had sent for from a glossy magazine; the mock sheepskin rug on the hearth; and the vase of dried flowers in the grate. This was an ambitious mother. He nodded to the sergeant, who went out.

'Mary was on her own, I believe, this afternoon?' asked Coward.

'She was used to it,' said Jean defensively. 'I'm home by six. Sometimes she goes to a friend or to her granny's. On schooldays she has homework, and then there are her piano lessons.'

'Oh – learning the piano, is she?'

'Yes. She likes it. She's a good girl, Inspector.'

'I'm sure she is,' answered Coward. 'Now then, she went to Miss Price at five o'clock.' He went over Mary's movements again. 'Miss Price says she was punctual, and left just before six. You were home soon after that, Mrs Forman?'

'Yes. The bus was on time. But it was raining hard. I got soaked coming from the square. I thought Mary would be at the Smiths' waiting till it stopped, so I didn't worry. She and Heather Smith were to have gone to Miss Price together.'

'Yes. So I understand,' said the chief inspector. 'You went out again yourself later on?'

'Yes. I had my tea; then it was time for the Wives' Club. I'm on the committee now,' Jean said.

'And you were out too, Mr Forman?'

'The caged birds,' explained Joe. Because of the rain he hadn't been able to put in his usual gardening spell; he'd had an extra few pints instead.

'I see. Well, if we don't find her as a result of the enquiries we're making tonight, we'll start a full-scale search at first light,' said the chief inspector. 'We can't do a lot while it's dark, as I'm sure you'll understand.'

At this point the sergeant returned, and shook his head when Coward glanced at him.

'Hm. She's not at her grandmother's, nor, as far as we can say, at any friend's in the village but there are still calls to be made. Now, have you a photograph of Mary?'

Mrs Forman could find only an old snap taken at the seaside a year ago with some other children.

'I see. Pity it's not more recent. But I expect a good many people in the village know her,' said the chief inspector. Wiveldown was still small enough for most of the inhabitants to recognise each other by sight, if not by name.

'I'm going to look for her,' Joe suddenly burst out. 'I can't sit here all night waiting. We ought to be searching, not talking.'

'We are searching,' said Coward. 'You won't do a bit of good going out now. You'd much better try to get some rest. You won't find anything while it's dark.'

'I might,' said Joe obstinately. 'I can't sit here and do

nothing. I know the fields and paths around. She might have gone off looking for blackberries on her way home.'

They could not dissuade him.

'We'll send a policewoman out to stay with you,' Chief Inspector Coward said to Jean.

'No – I'll be all right,' Jean said.

Her husband looked at her hard.

'You'll stay here,' he said. 'No going round next door, or that. Mary might come home.'

'I'll stay,' said Jean.

'Your mother's on her way, Mr Forman,' said Detective Sergeant Davis. 'She'll be here in five minutes.'

IV

After drinking his early morning cup of tea, Major Johnson opened the front door and stood on the porch inhaling deeply. The air smelt fresh, cleared by the storm which seemed to have moved completely away. On the other side of the road, and some way further down, he could see a police car parked outside the vicarage, and while he watched a policeman came out of the gates and walked up the path of the cottage next door. Almost at once the vicar's shabby old Ford Prefect, twelve years old, emerged and went off up the road, with the vicar crouched over the wheel and his white hair a nimbus about his head. A burglary, thought the major.

He returned indoors and had just spread a good lather all over his chin before he began shaving when his front door bell rang.

A policeman stood on the step.

'Good morning, sir. I'm sorry to disturb you so early but there's a child gone missing in the village and we're enquiring at every house to check her movements. Your name, sir, please?' said the constable.

Major Johnson supplied it. He dabbed the soapsuds off his chin.

'Who's missing?' he asked. 'I don't know many of the children by name.'

'It's an eleven-year-old girl, Mary Forman.' The constable produced a blown-up print of Mary's photograph made from the group her mother had found, but Major Johnson did not look at it.

'I know Mary Forman,' he said. 'I gave her a lift back from Leckington in my car yesterday. She was hitch-hiking. I scolded her for it.'

'What time was this, sir?' asked the constable.

'About two o'clock,' said Major Johnson.

'I see, sir. Perhaps I might come in a minute while I get the facts?'

'Certainly, constable,' said Major Johnson. He led the way into his sitting-room.

'Take a seat, constable,' said the major.

The constable sat down on an upright chair, his notebook open, and Major Johnson took one of the armchairs.

'Now, sir, exactly where did you pick Mary up?'

Major Johnson described his journey and how he had dropped Mary outside her grandmother's bungalow.

'I see, sir. And how did you know her name? Did she tell you?'

'No. Mary is one of the few children I do know. I was time-keeper at Walter's, where her father works, for some months. I've seen him with Mary about the place. What's happened to her?'

'We don't know, sir. She was last seen at six o'clock on the other side of the village.'

'I went up to The Grapes at about six-thirty – perhaps a little later. I often do in the evening. I didn't see Mary, though.' The major cudgelled his memory. 'No, there was no child about. It was raining then – there was a heavy storm. Perhaps she went to shelter somewhere?'

'That's what we must hope,' said the constable. 'Thank you, sir.'

'I hope you find her soon,' said Major Johnson. 'She was a very nice little girl.'

He showed the policeman out. His face felt tight from the dried soap on his chin, and he went back to the bathroom to spread a fresh lather over his beard.

Before getting back into the car, the alert constable made a note of the major's last remark.

V

The vicar went immediately round to the Formans' house as soon as the police left him. They were not churchgoers, but they were part of his flock and he must offer comfort if he could.

The Reverend Cedric Wilson was interested in early English madrigals, and it was a disappointment to him that no one in his parish, not even clever, devout Miss Price, shared this enthusiasm. He was also a keen ornithologist, and not unlike an eagle in appearance himself with his beaked nose and fine brow. He took an interest in the Brownies and had shown them his wildfowl slides, and he knew each child individually.

He found Jean Forman and her mother-in-law in the kitchen, with a pot of cold tea on the table between them and two untouched cups poured out. Both women were haggard; Jean had been crying and her face was blotched with tear stains.

Her face fell when she saw who the caller was.

'Oh – vicar – I thought it might be – ' she did not finish.

'I've just heard the news, Mrs Forman. You must be very anxious. But we must pray that Mary will be found safe and sound.'

'Would you like to come in? We're having some tea.'

Mrs Forman senior had braced up, rinsed out the teapot and put the kettle on again the moment the visitor arrived.

'Do you mind the kitchen?' Jean asked, offering him a chair.

The vicar's mind seldom dwelt on such mundane matters, but even he noticed how well equipped the Formans' kitchen was, not only compared with his own, which his sister when she came to stay called prehistoric, but compared with others he drank tea in on his rounds. Bright yellow cupboards lined the walls; black and white tiles covered the floor. The stainless steel sink gleamed.

The vicar knew Mrs Forman senior better than her daughter-in-law. She was a dressmaker, and his sister, every time she visited him, brought lengths of material for her to make up. He turned to her.

'I'm so sorry about this,' he said. 'The police told me Mary was with you during the afternoon.'

'Yes – for an hour. Then she went home to get ready for her Brownie test,' said Mrs Forman. She went through what Mary had done, as far as they knew it. 'Joe was out all night, searching. Of course he found nothing. The police have got men out now, in the fields, and dogs.'

'They'll find her. Perhaps she sheltered somewhere – in a shed, for instance – and fell asleep.'

'Joe knocked up every house between here and Miss Price's in the night,' said Jean. 'No one saw her after six o'clock. She bought some sweets at the post office just before five.'

'They might not have seen her pass on her way back,' said Mrs Forman. 'They'd have been closed by then.'

'Where's Joe now?' asked the vicar.

'Out with the police,' said Jean.

'He's had no rest, not a bite to eat, only some tea,' said his mother.

'I expect he feels he's helping, by joining the search,' said the Reverend Wilson.

'He blames me for going out,' said Jean, and began to weep again. She found a handkerchief in the sleeve of her dress and dabbed at her eyes.

'And do you blame yourself?' the vicar asked her, sitting down at the table. He accepted a cup of tea from the older woman with some relief; he had rushed out from the vicarage without any breakfast and his stomach had uttered a warning rumble; such an awkward noise at an emotional moment.

'I'd not have gone with her to Miss Price's, even if I'd been

53

at home,' said Jean. 'She was old enough to go alone. She was eleven.' Jean was using the past tense.

'She *is* eleven, Jean,' said Mrs Forman firmly. 'And that's old enough to go about the village by herself. But when she wasn't back at six, you should have looked for her, or waited here, and not gone out yourself.'

'Oh dear,' thought the vicar. 'Here's a coil.' Aloud he said, 'Now, let's not apportion blame today, when all we are concerned about is that Mary should be found, safe and well.'

He was still there, trying to restore domestic harmony, when Chief Inspector Coward arrived and told them that Mary had hitch-hiked back from Leckington the previous afternoon.

'Did she tell you she'd done that?' he asked the child's grandmother.

'No. I thought she'd come on the bus,' said Mrs Forman. 'Did she miss it?'

'No. Major Johnson came back before the bus. She told him she wanted to save the fare,' said the chief inspector.

'Now I come to think of it, she was early. She couldn't have come on the bus. I never noticed at the time,' said Mrs Forman.

'Well, it doesn't matter now. But it means that if she hitched a lift from Leckington, she might have gone in someone else's car.'

'Not a stranger's,' Jean insisted. 'She'd have recognised the major.'

'Mrs Forman, strangers can be plausible,' said the chief inspector. 'Unfortunately there was so much rain in the night that there's not much hope of picking up any scent of her. But we'll find something soon.'

I hope, he added, under his breath.

VI

There were two policemen in the car that stopped at Mrs Pollock's house. Mary had not shut the gate when she rushed out, and it swung on its hinge, creaking. They walked up the overgrown drive and rang the bell. When there was no reply they rang it a second time. Then they walked round to the back door. A cat-flap was let into it, and while they stood there a tabby cat pushed through it and sped past them into the bushes. There was a rinsed, empty milk bottle on the step. They didn't know that Mrs Pollock took a fresh pint only on alternate days.

'Owner away,' said one constable. 'The kid couldn't have come here, anyway. It's in the wrong direction altogether.'

His colleague peered in at the kitchen window. Everything looked orderly. The dishcloth, neatly draped over the sink, was just as Mary had left it. Mrs Pollock, dead in her chair, was invisible from where he stood.

The two policemen went away.

VII

Tom got out of the car, stumbled down the road and was sick into the ditch. He stood there, heaving and trembling, for some minutes, and all the time the rain poured down. That little kid. He saw the small hand slowly uncurling in his mind's eye. Where could she have sprung from? She must have moved right in front of the car when he turned to speak to Roger. Perhaps she was thumbing a lift.

What was he to do now?

He stood, irresolute, in the lane. Then he began to walk back the way he and Roger had come earlier. Where the road forked, he would take the other turn, no matter where it led. He couldn't think where Roger had vanished to, either. He needed him, to be told what to do. Roger led all their enterprises. But it was Roger's fault that this had happened. If he hadn't taken up Roger's challenge and stolen those boots in the market he wouldn't be here now, and that kid would still be alive. He began to sob, still half-drunk and very shocked, as he walked along, tears mingling with the rain on his face. His wiry hair got wetter and wetter and his soaked jeans clung to his legs.

That kid would be missed soon. The police would be out looking for her. And what about the geezer whose car that was? They'd be certain to catch up with him, and it would be all the harder for him if he'd hidden what he'd done.

But he walked on. After a long time he came to another village, really just a hamlet, a cluster of cottages and a farm-house near a cross-roads. Because of the rain the sky was dark now, though it was only nine o'clock. Tom was quite surprised to find his wristwatch still working. He stood at the cross-roads wondering which way to go, and as he hesitated a bus came along. He made up his mind and hailed it. He must get out of the rain.

There were only a few passengers. Tom bought a ticket to Leckington and went right to the back of the bus, where he sat huddled and shivering as it moved off. It was warm and dry, and his relief at being out of the storm was immense, but he couldn't stop shaking. The bus went into Wiveldown, and he shrank further back into his seat when it stopped in the square, his face turned away from the window. Two middle-aged women got on and sat a few seats in front of Tom. They had been spending the day in the village and carried polythene bags full of flowers and vegetables they had been given to take home. They never stopped talking throughout the journey.

Leckington was the end of the run. Everyone got out except Tom, in whom all thought had ceased. The driver-conductor roused him.

'Well, lad, all change here. We don't go any further,' he called genially.

Tom jerked into life.

'Oh – thanks,' he said and got out quickly.

'Goodnight, lad. Best get home and into some dry things,' said the driver, who recognised Tom as being a local boy but could put no name to him.

'I will. Ta,' said Tom.

But he couldn't go home, not yet. They'd all be about and they'd see that something was up. He went to Bert's Café and bought a cup of tea and a cake with the last of his money. Maybe he'd feel better with something inside him. He looked round anxiously in case Roger was in here too, but there was no sign of him.

The tea was hot and sweet and he gulped it down, but he gagged on the cake and couldn't swallow it. Two girls he knew came and sat at his table. Normally he would have chatted them up, but tonight he barely noticed them.

'Some folks is a bit too big for their boots, not saying can I buy you a coffee,' said one girl to her friend.

'It's a different story on Friday nights, flashing his money around and that,' said the other. 'But I forgot – he lost his job. Maybe we'll have to pay for him if we aren't careful.'

They continued to talk at him in this way. Tom heard some of the words but the sense washed over him. He got up and left the café without speaking to them.

'Looked awful, didn't he?' said one, when he had gone. 'Proper ill, and soaking wet.'

'Been out without his umbrella,' said the second, tittering.

They did not have to sit alone at their table for long. Soon two other boys came to join them. They forgot about Tom.

The tea had stopped him shivering, but he began again as soon as he went out into the street. He couldn't go home yet. His mum and dad would still be up. His dad would want to know whether he'd been along to the labour, and if they'd sent him after a job. His mother would look solemn about his wet clothes and start to fuss. His sisters would be watching television or giggling together if they weren't out with their boy-friends. If he went straight up to his room he'd just lie on his bed and see that kid again. Fair hair, she had. She had on a Brownie dress. His sisters had been Brownies, centuries ago.

He walked the streets till after midnight, when he knew his parents would be in bed and asleep. Then he went home and let himself in quietly by the back door.

VIII

Although he told Tom that Mary must have been walking in the road, Roger was not sure that this was so. He had been looking ahead when he blew the horn and there was no sign of her; and she must have heard them coming. When Tom went off to turn the car he saw a gap in the hedge at the side of the road; there was a stile there, and a sign which pointed to a public footpath. He was over in a flash and loping across the field beyond.

Mary, in fact, once clear of Mrs Pollock's house, had taken a short cut across the fields; the road looped round in a semicircle but the other way cut several hundred yards from the journey home. In spite of the rain, Mary had known the way. Roger had no such local knowledge; he missed the second stile and came to a gate. It was securely wired up, so he climbed it and crossed the next field. There were some heifers in it; they looked at him, puffed and snorted, and came to investigate the intruder, one of them lowing loudly. Roger ran as fast as he could away from them, and they set off in lumbering, interested, harmless pursuit. He got across the next gate and leaned against it, panting, while they blew at him from their side, disappointed at being foiled in these friendly overtures.

Warily, he set off again; however, there were no livestock in this field. But there was a shed.

It offered shelter, for the rain was pouring down. Roger went into it and stood huddled in a corner waiting for the storm to pass and trying to think straight. Putting the child in the boot of the car had been an instinctive action with him, a bid for time, but she'd be found soon, and that git Tom would crack. Well, it had nothing to do with him. Tom had driven the car and his prints would be on the wheel. But Roger's would be in the car too. He didn't want any part of a murder rap, and that's what it would be, for sure.

He must get away, out of the district, to London, or maybe to the north. He'd make for the motorway and hitch a lorry.

He'd still got a pound or two, and with luck he'd nick a bit more somewhere on the way. But he mustn't risk running into Tom again.

He waited till it was nearly dark and then he struck off once more over the fields, glad to leave the shed which smelt of cow-dung. He'd lost all sense of direction, but he met no more cattle, and at last he reached a road.

He had trudged along it for only a hundred yards when he heard a car behind him and saw its lights approaching. He raised his thumb, and the car stopped. It was driven by a plump young man with a fair moustache.

'I'm going to Bletchford. Any good?' he asked.

'It's on my way,' said Roger. 'Thanks.'

IX

Chief Inspector Coward's men, searching the fields for Mary, found two abandoned bicycles early on Friday morning. They were not missed from the farm until two hours later, when their loss was reported at once.

The sergeant at the desk in Leckington police station took the details down over the telephone. The matter did not seem to be connected with Mary's disappearance, and every available constable was out searching for her; the theft of two bicycles, though tiresome, did not at that moment seem an urgent matter, but Superintendent Harris heard about it as he passed the desk on his way out to the temporary police headquarters in the school in Wiveldown. When he got out there and discovered that the bicycles had been found he thought there might be some link; one was quite a small machine. Detective Sergeant Davis and a constable were sent to Mordwell right away to see the farmer, Mr Bryant.

Mordwell had not so far been included in the house-to-house search for Mary because it was six miles from where she lived, but as no trace of her had yet been found the range would have to be extended. Already the first reporters had arrived, and soon appeals would be made in the press, on radio and television.

Mr Bryant grew vegetables on a large scale; he had contracts with a canning factory for peas and beans, and he owned five greengrocery shops. When he had a glut of produce, he sold the surplus off in the market, and this Thursday he had had several hundred cabbages and marrows to dispose of which would rot if left.

'Quick work, sergeant, finding the bikes so soon,' he said.

'I'm afraid you can't have them back just yet,' said Sergeant Davis. 'We want to look for prints on them.'

'Oh, why bother? You say they aren't damaged. Let's forget it this time. I'm sure you've enough to do. Probably just some kid's prank.'

'I expect so, sir. I hope you're right,' said the sergeant. 'But there's a child missing in Wiveldown, an eleven-year-old girl. There could be a connection. We'll let you have them back as soon as possible.'

'Good. My boys want to go off fishing – they're on holiday now, bike for miles, they do.'

'It'll be a day or two, sir,' said the sergeant.

'Hum. What do you think has happened to the child?'

'Can't say, yet, sir. So far we haven't found a sign of her.'

'Sounds bad, eh?'

'Yes. But we must hope she's safe. Children sometimes turn up after several days, having hidden in barns and so forth.'

'I've got a barn. Do you want to have a look at it?' asked Bryant. 'It's a long walk, though, from Wiveldown.'

'I would like to see it, yes. Is that where you kept the cycles?'

'No – they were in another shed with the tractor. It's out, in fact, I left it in the yard, but it was raining cats and dogs when I got back from market yesterday and I didn't bother to put it away.'

He led the two policemen to the barn. The truck was there, just as he had left it. Sergeant Davis put out a hand to stop Bryant from walking up to it.

'Just a minute, sir,' he said, looking down at the ground.

The tyre marks of the truck showed clearly in the dust, and there, sharply defined near the entrance to the barn, was a footprint.

'Not yours, Mr Bryant,' said the sergeant, looking down at the farmer's huge foot. 'One of your men, perhaps. Anyone been in here since you got back from market?'

'No. I've got two men who work for me, but they haven't been up here today.'

The constable had disappeared further into the barn and was poking about at the back, near the stacks of hay. He came forward. In his hand, held gingerly in a handkerchief between finger and thumb, was an empty bottle of Bristol Cream Sherry.

X

Miss Price rose as usual at half-past six. She had slept only intermittently since the police had called the night before; they had checked her account of Mary's visit and then left. Miss Price had tried to convince herself that Mary must have wandered into someone's garden shed seeking shelter from the storm and got locked in, but it seemed unlikely. The rain did not begin till after she had gone; the walk home should have taken only ten or fifteen minutes – even if she dawdled along and picked some more flowers she could not have taken more than half-an-hour. Miss Price had shown the policemen the daisies Mary had brought for her; she had put them in a pottery jug on the window-sill, where they stood now, bright and glowing.

Outside the house sunlight shone on the rain-soaked grass and all the flowers in the garden hung wet heads. Miss Price went round her garden talking aloud, as she often did.

'What can have happened to Mary?' she asked the hollyhocks. Then she fed the budgerigar and asked him too. After that she made a pot of tea and drank two cups, and ate three digestive biscuits. By then it was half-past seven: still too early to visit the Formans, she supposed. Her habitual early rising meant a lot of hanging about waiting for the rest of the world to wake up and start the day.

She recited aloud the first twenty stanzas of how, according to Lord Macaulay, Horatius held the bridge. Then she wheeled out her bicycle. Though she was nearly seventy she still rode round the district for miles on her old-fashioned machine. She kept it well maintained, and until recently had mended all her own punctures, but lately the young man next door had been doing this for her. He had seen her once with her bucket of water finding the hole in the tube; intrigued, he'd watched over the fence and asked to be taught how to do it, so that he need not take his own small boy's cycle to the garage. Silently marvelling that a generation could grow up so helpless, Miss Price had taught him what to do. Since he had so much time to make up, and needed to keep his hand in, she gave him her own repairs now.

She rode off, dressed in a baggy skirt and thick stockings. A few cars taking people to work passed her, and she saw the square was active; a police van was outside the school, and two police cars were parked beside it. Several people stood some distance from them, staring. She pedalled past The Grapes, where all the curtains were still drawn; the Hursts kept late hours, and she felt tolerant towards them, knowing they must be washing up far into the night, although in her opinion people who lay in bed on summer mornings missed the best of the day.

She turned into Welbeck Crescent and met the vicar's car coming towards her. He stopped when he saw her, and she dismounted from her machine. The vicar realised where she was going.

'Is there any news?' she asked him.

'Not yet.'

He told her how Mary had hitched a lift from Major Johnson. 'It means she might go in someone else's car,' he said.

'Oh, do you think so? Wouldn't she go only with someone she knew?' Miss Price shared the same optimistic view of Mary's likely conduct as her mother.

'No one she knew would be likely to offer her a lift out of the village,' pointed out the vicar reasonably enough. 'Alternatively, even one's acquaintances may unfortunately go beserk.'

'You really think something terrible may have happened?'

'Don't you?' the vicar asked.

'I find it hard to explain why she wasn't home soon after leaving me, certainly,' said Miss Price. 'And she couldn't have had an accident in the village without anyone knowing. But we must hope there's another explanation.'

'I'm glad you're going there,' said the vicar. 'Joe's just come back. He's been up all night searching for the child and out with the police this morning. He's blaming Jean for not staying at home.'

'And he's quite right, though she can't be held wholly responsible for this,' said Miss Price. 'Jean always had a lot of silly ideas, even as a child. She was bright – I taught her, you know—but her values were all wrong. She was lucky to marry Joe. He's a good, kind man, but not ambitious enough for her. I'll get on up there, vicar.'

With that, she mounted her bicycle again and pedalled off. The vicar had forgotten that she had known Jean Forman from childhood. She would take this tragedy, if it proved to be one, as a personal disaster, but she might put some of her own forthright spirit into Jean Forman. Miss Price had, as a girl, played hockey for Somerset, and she was still equal to a battle.

At the Formans' house, Joe was having a bath and his mother was cooking him bacon and eggs. Jean was industriously vacuuming the living-room. Miss Price marched straight in upon her.

'Well, Jean,' she said. 'Switch that thing off and sit down. You won't bring Mary back by polishing.'

'I can't sit still,' said Jean, but she obeyed.

'Very likely not. But you can try, while we talk. Now, has Mary any special places where she likes to go? Secret haunts? Children do.'

'Not that I know of.' Jean looked surprised. 'Why?'

'She was alone a lot. She didn't always stay here waiting for you in the empty house, I'm sure. I met her once up at the old chalk-pit when I was out for a ramble.'

Miss Price made constant long-distance rambles on foot or by bicycle, devising the plots of her books, and was a well-known local sight on this account.

'The old chalk pit?'

'Yes. On the Chorlbury road. I told the police I'd seen her there. They're searching it.'

'I didn't know she'd ever been there,' said Jean.

'She said her father took her once. This time she was alone. She remembered it as a nice place, full of wild flowers – that's why she'd gone back there. I brought her back to the village with me,' said Miss Price. 'I made her promise not to go there alone again without telling someone. She'd keep her word, I think.'

'Yes, she would,' Jean said. 'She was – is – very obedient.'

But she'd gone for a ride in the major's car.

'So I wondered if there were any other spots she might go to, like the chalk-pit,' Miss Price pursued. 'But if there were, you wouldn't know about them, would you?'

Jean shook her head.

'I don't think you know her at all,' said Miss Price. 'You're out of the house so much, when you're at home you must be too busy to talk to your family. When do you do your house-work? I must say, you keep the place immaculate. Mind you, I'm not against you working, Jean. I'm in favour of it. But not if your family suffers. You could have found a part-time job, or something in the village. Mrs Hurst at The Grapes is always short-handed.'

'Domestic work,' said Jean.

'You meet people in a pub,' said Miss Price.

Jean stiffened and looked at her. Miss Price was regarding her steadily with the same intense gaze that had caught her cheating as a child.

'I suppose you were at the Wives' Club last night. It can be checked. But the meetings end well before ten, I know – usually nine-thirty. I've talked at them. I wonder where you went on the way home. You didn't miss Mary till nearly eleven o'clock.'

Miss Price stood up and looked down at Jean, who had not answered.

'You were always a muddled thinker, Jean. I sincerely pray that Mary will be found. It's much too soon to give up hope. But sort your priorities out, my dear.'

She swept regally from the house, and as she rode off down the road the sound of the vacuum cleaner could be heard again, through the open window.

Bicycles travel silently, and one summer evening not so long ago when Miss Price was returning from visiting a friend she had seen Jean Forman in a grey car that was parked in a gateway. The man with her had lighted a cigarette, illuminating both their faces, as Miss Price rode noiselessly past.

Superintendent Harris and Chief Inspector Coward were conferring together outside the temporary police headquarters in the school when Miss Price passed on her way home. She stopped to ask for news, explaining who she was.

'Ah yes – the last person to see Mary, as far as we know,' said the superintendent. He was a tall man with clearly marked black eyebrows and a strong face. Miss Price took to him at once. If it was possible to find Mary alive, or alternatively if anyone had harmed her and must be brought to book, this man would see that it was done. 'We've found nothing yet,' he told her.

'You've searched the chalk-pit?'

'Some men with a dog are up there now.'

But none of them really thought that Mary had gone all that way in a thunderstorm. Not voluntarily.

When Miss Price had gone, Superintendent Harris said:

'This report of a pair of boots stolen from a market-stall yesterday – get on to it. There might be a link with the bicycles, though it seems a long shot. Abducting little girls isn't usually in the line of tearaway youths, but we'd better make sure, one way or the other. I don't like the smell of this case at all.'

XI

Major Johnson went out to pick runner beans at the bottom of his garden. He had a good crop of them, and they were just at their peak; he could not eat them all himself. They twined luxuriantly round the tall poles, orange flowers high up the stems and clusters of slender beans among the leaves. He stripped off all that were ripe and then stepped over to the hedge which divided him from the Blunts. Cathy should soon be pegging out her washing. By standing on an upturned tub the major could look over the top and call to her.

Cathy was there. He could see her corn-coloured hair and blue dress.

'Mrs Blunt,' he called.

'Oh – Major Johnson!' Cathy always called him the Cheshire Cat because his face usually appeared grinning above her suddenly, like this. They seldom met in more conventional situations. 'Hullo!'

'Would you like some beans?'

'Yes, please.'

'I've picked a lot. Got your basket?'

Cathy always stood on a garden seat which the Blunts had on the further side of the hedge and held up a basket to receive the bounty from next door.

'No – I'll get it – or why don't you come round?' It was ridiculous that the old boy had never been inside their house; she'd kept saying to Derek that they must ask him in, and Derek had agreed, but what with the baby arriving and one thing and the other, they had never done it. And this morning she felt upset; the police, arriving just after she had fed her baby, with such a distressing reason for their call, had disturbed her. It would be nice to talk to someone. Miss Amanda Blunt was only six weeks old and not yet very chatty. 'Come round and have some coffee,' she invited.

'Oh, thank you. That's most kind,' said Major Johnson. He was delighted.

He dismounted from his perch, rubbed his hand over his wisps of hair to flatten them, and walked round promptly, feeling a little shy but very pleased. He liked the Blunts but felt awkward if they met; they were so very young. And Cathy had been so conspicuously pregnant that he'd felt embarrassed; a friendship over the hedge was about their limit, he'd accepted.

'The police must have come to you too, I suppose,' said Cathy as she carried the cups on to the paved terrace outside the sitting-room.

'Yes, they did. I gave Mary a lift back from Leckington yesterday,' said the major, and told the tale again.

'I don't know her,' Cathy said. 'But it's awful. You hear of such dreadful things these days. They could happen even in Wiveldown.' She gazed anxiously at the pram, parked in the shade, where Amanda lay peacefully sleeping. Major Johnson had duly admired her before he sat down, though very little of her – a minute ear and the top of a small head covered in golden fluff – was visible from under her wraps. What threats lay in store for her daughter, Cathy thought worriedly.

'Mary must be safe,' said the major. 'She was so near home. I'm sure she'll soon be found.'

'I wonder if Ruth Fellowes met her,' said Cathy. 'She came to tea – she left not long before the storm began, she must have got caught in it. Do you know Ruth?'

'Yes, indeed,' said the major, and was about to tell her that he had taken Mrs Fellowes home the night before when he changed his mind. He had left her house rather late; she was a lady living alone, and Major Johnson was an old-fashioned man who had lived abroad a lot and not kept pace with contemporary life in Britain. Though it was impossible to imagine Mrs Fellowes in compromising circumstances, people's tongues were long and he did not wish to cause her any embarrassment. So he kept silent.

'Why is your house called Tobruk, Major Johnson?' Cathy asked him, biting into a ginger biscuit.

He looked at her, amazed. Could she be so young that she didn't know?

He told her.

XII

Ruth Fellowes was still asleep when the police knocked at her door. She looked out of the window to see who was below, then hastily pulled on her dressing-gown and dabbed at her springy grey hair with a brush before hurrying down.

She knew Mary. Just as Miss Price tested the Brownies for literacy, so did she for their cooking and hostess badges. Mary had already earned both.

'How dreadful,' she said. 'I didn't see her last night – I was out in the village at about half-past six. I went to see Mrs Blunt in Church Street, and I was walking back when the storm broke, so I went into The Grapes, for shelter. I had a drink too,' she added.

'I see.' The constable wrote it down. 'We'll just take a look round your garden, madam, if you don't mind. Have you a shed?'

She had.

'By all means, constable,' she said. 'But Miss Price lives on the other side of the village. How could Mary have wandered this way?'

'It doesn't seem likely that she did, but we must check everywhere,' said the policemen.

'Of course,' said Ruth.

Their search was soon over. When they had gone she dressed and had breakfast, then walked down to the post office for her newspaper. Because her cottage was in an isolated position no delivery boy could be found to go there, so she and the few other people who lived in that lane had to fetch their own.

She scarcely noticed the clear, sparkling weather for she was so shocked about Mary's disappearance. There had been no sign of her about when she had been with Major Johnson in his car, but anyone would take shelter in such a torrential downpour.

It had been a pleasant evening and she had enjoyed Major Johnson's company. Like many large women, Ruth was inwardly rather timid and she had spent most of her adult life acquiring a manner to match her bulk. Her husband had known how she felt, but he was large too. She guessed that Major Johnson had the same problem in reverse; he must be sensitive about being so small. But he was not in the least aggressive, as many small men were. She had admired his tenacity at the cookery classes, for he made valiant efforts to keep up with the other pupils who all started off with more basic knowledge than he had. Celia Mainwaring had laughed about him. 'One of my protégés,' she had said, and wondered what subject he should pursue next. He had talked so naturally last night about his army life, and then, when a huge spider had sauntered across the sitting-room floor, he had risen, gathered it up in one square, capable hand, and put it out of the window.

'I don't expect you like them,' he said. 'Most ladies don't. But I never kill them – not in this country, anyway. Some people think it's unlucky.'

Ruth, who quite liked spiders, melted into her chair feeling about five feet two inches tall, and as warm as if she had swallowed a double brandy. He was a kind, unassuming man, and he was lonely. She resolved that he should bring her back from Chorlbury Manor in future, instead of boring Madge Fazackerley.

The two Mrs Flints, Deirdre and Marilyn, who ran the post office and sold the papers, were forty and forty-two years old, and both weighed over eleven stone. The two brothers they had married managed a haulage contractor's business while their childless wives gossiped away the day, not with their customers but with each other, occasionally interrupting their chat to pay pensions or sell stamps. As they never tired of explaining, they sold the newspapers just to oblige, since no one else in the village would take it on. While they talked together, the two Mrs Flints knitted. Vast sweaters in elaborate lacy patterns poured from their needles, and woe betide the customer who expected to be served in the middle of a row.

But today the knitting still lay furled in its plastic bags beside each lady. The two plump faces, thickly plastered with pan cake make-up and with carmine lips beneath helmets of stiff black hair, gazed avidly out over the counter, the two huge busts leaned on the rounded arms while their owners surmised what fate had befallen Mary.

Like Mary, Ruth Fellowes was not fond of these two, but she said her usual cheerful 'Good morning', to them both.

'I'll take my paper, shall I?' she said, and went to help herself from the pile of *Daily Telegraphs*.

'I'll get it for you, Mrs Fellowes.' The slightly fatter Mrs Flint came round from behind the counter and, with dampened thumb, sorted through the pile till she came to the one with Mrs Fellowes' name on it.

'Oh – thank you.' This was unaccustomed attention.

'Terrible about little Mary Forman, isn't it?' said Mrs Flint the larger.

'Has she been found?' asked Ruth.

'Not yet – but it's obvious, isn't it? I mean to say –'

'What's obvious?' asked Ruth in a voice like steel.

'Stands to reason,' said the second Mrs Flint.

'What does?' asked Ruth ominously.

'She'll have been murdered of course, poor little mite, and her in here only last evening buying some sweets.'

'I hope you're wrong, Mrs Flint,' said Ruth. 'She's probably wandered off somewhere and will turn up perfectly safely.'

At this point another customer arrived: Major Johnson, in smart grey flannels and navy blazer.

'Ah, good morning, Mrs Fellowes.' His smile was tempered with reserve, for all Wiveldown must be grave today. He nodded to the Mesdames Flint. 'May I take my paper?'

'We've no boy today, major,' said Deirdre Flint. She plucked out Major Johnson's *Daily Mail*. 'We were just saying, isn't it sad about Mary?'

'She's been found?' asked the major.

'No,' said Ruth. 'There isn't any news.'

'But we all know what will have happened,' said Marilyn.

'Some maniac, it must be. These wicked men.' She shuddered greedily.

'I don't think we should assume the worst yet, Mrs Flint,' said the major firmly. 'Think how such talk would distress her family. There must still be hope that she's safe.'

'I quite agree, Major Johnson,' said Ruth. 'It's very worrying, but it's too soon yet to fear the worst.'

'It's always the same in these cases,' said Deirdre. 'Several days pass, and then the kiddies' bodies turn up, marked by dreadful wounds.'

'Mrs Flint, you must not talk like that,' said the major. 'Only a few weeks ago a missing child was found asleep and unharmed in a wood, somewhere in Hampshire. There must be other children in the village, Mary's friends, who could be needlessly upset if they knew that older people feared for Mary's life, not to mention her parents.'

'I quite agree with you, Major Johnson,' said Ruth. 'We must all hope that Mary will be found unharmed in the next few hours.' She stalked out of the post office on these words, followed by the major, and the two Mrs Flints looked at one another and shrugged.

'Well, I don't know! Some people,' said one.

'A little too big for our boots today, aren't we?' said the other.

Outside the post office Ruth Fellowes turned to Frederick Johnson, looking down at him with a solemn expression.

'I'm glad you said that. Those two are like the *tricoteuses* by the guillotine,' she said. 'They give me the creeps. But I'm horribly afraid they may be right about Mary.'

'So am I,' said Major Johnson. The two of them looked across the square to where a police car was parked; beside it, two men in plain clothes were talking to a uniformed sergeant in the road, and another policeman, radio squawking, came up on his motor-cycle as they watched. 'Mrs Flint and her sister are like the ghouls who go to accidents and goggle at the victims. Not the nicest people in the village.'

'No,' said Ruth.

71

'That was a very pleasant evening,' said the major. 'Thank you so much for your hospitality.'

'You must come again,' said Ruth.

'I'd like to,' said the major. 'Well, I must be off.' He smiled at her again and turned away.

Ruth smiled too. She was still smiling when she reached her own house.

XIII

Surprisingly, once his shivering ceased, Tom slept; but when morning came and the bustle of his father and sisters getting ready for work began, he pulled the bedclothes up over his head, curled himself into a foetal bundle, and remained there, motionless, until successive bangs of the back door announced their departure. The house then echoed to the clatter of his mother, down in the kitchen, and the syphoning sound of the water system refilling.

He got up, flung on a pair of jeans and a sweater, and his plimsolls which were still damp, and rushed out of the house. His mother heard him, but she was too late to catch him. She went up to his room and sighed over the disorder she found there: the sheets and blankets were dragged off the bed and pulled on to the floor, and under them was a pile of discarded clothes. She picked them up; they were soaking wet, and had made the sheets damp too. She took them down to wash.

Until the garage closed and he lost his job, Tom had always been such a good boy; he was quiet and gentle, not at all like his noisy sisters, and she hoped he was set for a good career in the motor trade. Now he idled about from day to day and she never knew who he mixed with. His sisters said he went to that rough Bert's Café, which they wouldn't be seen dead in; all the town's yobbos went there, and it was not the sort of place Mrs West thought her son should frequent. She had lain awake last night, worrying, until she heard him come in. He was seldom out so late, and he had never gone off like this in the morning without a word, and without a bite to eat.

Tom, who had found some odd coins in his dry jeans, bought a *Daily Mirror*, expecting to see in enormous headlines, CHILD'S BODY FOUND IN BOOT OF CAR, but the main story was an alleged case of bribery in the police, and though he scanned the paper thoroughly there was nothing about a missing child in it. Next, he went to where Roger lived in a terraced house on the edge of the town. Roger's mother was a thin, drawn widow, always exhausted, who worked as a cleaner; she was afraid of Roger, who treated her almost as badly as his father had done. She had already left for work when Tom arrived, and there was no sign of Roger; the house was empty.

Leckington was always busy on Fridays, but that day there were several police cars among the traffic; one went through the town with its light flashing and its siren sounding. Tom heard two women with shopping bags on their arms speculating about the cause of the activity. While he listened a third woman came and told them that a child was missing somewhere in the district.

'Murdered, most like,' said the woman, and Tom felt sick to his stomach.

He wandered about for a while, without an aim, and then he walked up and down outside the police station wondering whether to go in and tell them what had happened. It was an accident. He hadn't meant any harm to the kid, he never saw her. But whose was the car? It wasn't one he recognised from his days at the garage. Maybe it came from far away. It would look bad for the poor bugger whose car it was when the child was found.

After walking about for a couple of hours in a confused state, Tom went up to the labour exchange where he was told of a job as a loader and cleaner at the paint factory. Not his style at all, he'd have said the day before. But now he set off to apply for it, determined to get it, no matter how dull the work and whatever the wage.

XIV

Major Johnson turned on the radio for the one o'clock news while he ate a quick snack before going to Chorlbury Manor for his afternoon's duty. After the political news there was an announcement about the missing child and she was described.

The Manor opened at two o'clock and Admiral Bruce liked all the staff to be there in plenty of time. Major Johnson was often the first to arrive. His route lay past the square, and today a small crowd had collected outside the school. As he drove out of the village he saw a group of policemen in rubber boots, twenty or more, coming towards him. Several were leading dogs. Some men with cameras, newspapermen he supposed, were among them. What a terrible business.

He reached the Manor and parked in the courtyard reserved for the staff. Then he walked round to the forecourt. Admiral Bruce was already there, pacing up and down as if on the quarter-deck. He hailed the major.

'Ah – Major Johnson. If you're not in a hurry this evening I'd be most grateful if you'd spare a few minutes after we close. I want to consult you,' he said.

'Certainly, admiral,' said Major Johnson.

'Splendid,' said the admiral, sketching a gesture in the air with his hand.

Major Johnson fought the desire which always attacked him when in the presence of the admiral to come to attention and salute. The admiral looked benign and his own conscience was clear; he was not being summoned to any parade of defaulters. He went into the house and began to prepare for the afternoon's intake of visitors. He liked this time, with the vast house hushed and expectant; the air of spacious repose was soothing. The major would have liked to live there when the house was at the height of its splendour, with servants scurrying round bringing comfort to the magnificently dressed occupants. But then, in those days, he would have been a servant, the major had to remind himself, at the very best a senior groom. At least now he was able to experience a little vicarious gracious living, seated in the linenfold-panelled hall at his ancient oak table, selling the tickets.

Fridays were always busy; today there were several coach-loads of Americans and a party of Danes, and a women's outing whose members were all a little too old to enjoy the stairs and the long passages, but who collapsed with delight over their special tea served in the orangery. But the day came to an end eventually and when the last visitor had gone and the house had been searched and locked, Ruth Fellowes came into the hall. Major Johnson was checking his day's takings, which were above average.

'The admiral wants to see me,' the major told her. 'Some matter he wants to discuss. Excuse me.'

He left her, looking pleased and important, and Ruth sighed. Madge Fazackerley it must be, after all.

Major Johnson found the admiral in his office with whisky and soda beside him on a tray. He poured out a drink for the major and bade him sit down, then came straight to the point. The Manor was becoming more popular every year and new attractions were constantly being added. He needed help with administration, especially the book-keeping.

'You'd be just the man for it, Major Johnson,' said the admiral. 'I want a man for this job – we've enough women about the place as it is. You'd be my deputy, my number one, you might say.' He wondered if the other would appreciate this naval allusion. Then he went on to name a salary.

The major could hardly believe his luck. The job would be almost full-time and very well paid. In the winter, when the house was closed, there were its maintenance and repairs to be dealt with. It would be interesting, worthwhile work of the kind he excelled at.

'Think it over,' said the admiral.

But the major needed no time to reflect.

'I'll be proud to accept,' he declared.

His one thought as he drove home was to wonder how soon he would be able to tell Miss Mainwaring this news. The money,

75

too, would make a great difference to how he lived; small luxuries would be everyday matters now, not rare extravagances. He wove a daydream in which he took her to dine at The Lamb and she said to him, over champagne, 'It's only what you deserve, Frederick, after your lifetime of experience'.

XV

That evening Major Johnson went up to The Grapes for his usual pint. He felt buoyant. At last he was adapting to civilian life and finding a niche. He had a job; he was on friendly terms with his young neighbours; he had a plan for the future. For a short while he forgot all about Mary, but he found the familiar bar at the pub full of strangers and was reminded at once of the tragedy. The press was here in force.

It was good for trade. Mr and Mrs Hurst were serving pints without pause.

Major Johnson fought his way through the mob to the bar counter and ordered his usual.

'Ah, major. Good evening,' said Mr Hurst.

'You're busy,' said Major Johnson. He, greeted personally, belonged in this pub, unlike all these strangers who would be gone for ever as soon as the excitement died down. He was warmed by the thought.

'Yes. One person's misfortune is another's good luck,' said Mr Hurst.

'Still no news?'

'Not a bit, I believe. Dreadful, isn't it? Most of the men in the village are turning out with the police tomorrow to go over the ground again.'

The landlord turned from him to attend to somebody else, and Major Johnson was buttonholed by a brisk man with a large moustache.

'Live here, do you?' he asked abruptly.

'I do,' answered Major Johnson.

76

'Did you know Mary Forman?'

'I do know Mary,' said the major.

'Seen her lately?'

'Yesterday afternoon,' said the major.

'Know the family?'

Major Johnson knew Joe from his days at the paint factory; he had heard about his wife's aspirations, but he did not propose to gratify the reporter's curiosity.

'Telling your readers a lot of tittle-tattle about the family won't help to find Mary, will it?' he said tartly. 'Print her picture, ask anyone who saw her yesterday to come forward – that's what you should do. But spare the family's feelings.'

'Well said, Major Johnson,' said a feminine voice. Penny Hurst had appeared in the bar. She still wore her drab long dress, but now she carried a rucksack and was with a pale young man wearing an orange shirt. 'Goodbye.' She drifted away, her companion following behind her, and Major Johnson remembered that she was going camping in Greece. What unsuitable clothes for life under canvas, he thought.

'Who's that?' asked the reporter.

'My daughter,' said Mr Hurst.

The reporter hurried out after the couple and there were noisy sounds of argument from the road. Finally there came the roar of a car's exhaust and the reporter returned, grinning.

'Camera shy, your daughter,' he told the landlord.

'Why do you want her photograph, for heaven's sake?' asked Mr Hurst.

'Human interest. Writing up the village for the Sundays,' said the reporter.

The certainty that Mary had met some terrible fate was with them all. They were like vultures, the newspapermen, waiting for the kill, thought the major. Doubtless they'd been hounding the wretched Formans all day. He finished his pint, his earlier elation gone.

After he left, the reporter who had talked to him, and who had heard Penny address him, made a careful note of his name. He did not take kindly to snubs.

XVI

Saturday's newspapers had the news about Mary's disappearance on the front pages, and they all carried an enlargement of the indifferent snapshot her mother had produced. Some had shots of the council house in Welbeck Crescent. DISTRAUGHT MOTHER, said one, with a picture of Jean. FATHER SEARCHES ALL NIGHT, said another.

Over her orange juice, grape nuts and coffee, Celia Mainwaring read *The Guardian's* precise account of the situation. She could not remember coming across either the child or her parents in the library; probably they did not read, or used the mobile van. She drank a second cup of coffee and then departed for the library wearing a new biscuit-coloured linen skirt and pale shirt, with a row of silver bangles on her wrist.

Saturday mornings were always busy, for the library closed at twelve and did not open again until Tuesday morning; there were dozens of customers changing their books for the weekend and Celia was late in closing. She hurried home with not much time to spare before she must be at the tennis club for a match in the afternoon, and found on her doorstep a large blue hydrangea in a pot. It was wrapped in florist's paper and a card in a neat, crabbed hand said: *With kind regards, Frederick Johnson. P.S. I have some good news to tell you.*

For a moment Miss Mainwaring wondered who Frederick Johnson was; then the major's round, always rather anxious-looking face swam into her mind's eye. She began to rock with laughter. What on earth could he want to tell her? That he'd been elected to the parish council?

In a lull at the match, during which Leckington Ladies made a bold stand against their opponents from across the county, she sat sunning her sturdy legs and told Mavis Combe, her partner, what had happened.

'Made a conquest, have you? What's he like?' Mavis enquired.

'Oh – tedious, and knee-high to a grasshopper,' Celia said. 'Silly old fool.'

'Watch out for fireworks,' Mavis said, giggling.

Tom West read the newspaper headline over his father's shoulder at breakfast. Now that he had a job he was trying to behave normally at home. He had watched television the night before and seen pictures of the search for Mary, and of her parents and her grandmother. So the child was still undiscovered. What could have happened to the car? Maybe the owner had found the kid, panicked, and dumped her somewhere miles away. It's what he would have done. When his father put the paper down he picked it up, trying to look casual. *My daughter wouldn't accept a lift from a stranger, sobs thirty-five-year-old heartbroken mother*, he read. There was a picture of Miss Price on her bicycle with the caption: *Well-known novelist the last to see Mary – is she alive?*

'It's terrible what the papers do,' said Tom's mother. 'That poor woman.'

'Must have been done in,' said one of Tom's sisters. 'Poor kid – some loony must have got her, I s'pose, like you was always warning us, mum.'

'Poor little sod,' said Tom, and burst out of the room. They heard him rush upstairs and a few minutes later came the sound of the lavatory flushing.

'What's with him?' asked the second sister.

'Leave him alone, you two,' said their mother.

Later, Tom went to Roger's house again. Mrs Brewis was there on her own. She had not seen Roger since Thursday morning, nor heard a word from him, but that was nothing new. He often vanished for weeks at a time and then reappeared just as suddenly, sometimes with a wad of money but more often broke.

Roger himself was in Birmingham when he read the paper. He had hitch-hiked there in three stages and spent last night in a hostel. So the kid hadn't been found yet. That was a lucky break. But he'd better get further away. He'd find a job for a week or two to put him in funds, and he'd look for some new mates. By then the trouble would all have died down. He must just hope that creep Tom West would keep his mouth shut.

Major Johnson had to walk to the post office once more for his *Daily Mail*. He collected the Blunts' *Daily Telegraph* and the *Express* for the Philpots, and said shortly to the Mrs Flints that he hoped the paper boy would soon be back.

One of the papers had a picture of the elder Mrs Flint on its middle page. *Sold sweets to missing child*, ran the text, and an interview with Deirdre was printed below. Marilyn was put out because she had not been featured and determined that when Mary was found her views would be given full publicity. Both ladies had intended to show this report to the major, since it was not in his paper, but when they saw the glint in his blue eyes they changed their minds.

'Looked ever so fierce, he did,' they said to one another, and repeated it to anyone who would listen in the days that followed.

XVII

Major Johnson had sent the hydrangea on a sudden impulse, inspired by seeing some flowers delivered to Cathy Blunt next door. It was her birthday, she told him later over the fence.

When was Miss Mainwaring's, he wondered.

But he need not wait for a special occasion to send her some; why not do it now? Taking her out to lunch had marked the start of his special campaign; flowers would consolidate the position gained by the first manœuvre. He drove into Leckington, arranged it all, finding Miss Mainwaring's address in the telephone directory, and drove back home in a state of euphoria. Then he took Cathy round a bunch of small early chrysanthemums, pink ones from his garden; the Blunts' garden was in the process of reorganisation, and Derek was out, stripped to the waist, guiding a rotavator over the ground among his apple trees.

The police were still active in the square as the major drove by on his way to the Manor that afternoon; patrol cars had been out during the morning asking through loudspeakers for anyone who had seen Mary on Thursday to come forward.

Several of the lady guides were arriving as the major drew up in his car. He saw Mrs Fellowes with Mrs Fazackerley get out of a green mini and go into the house ahead of him.

Admiral Bruce waylaid him as he walked across the fore-court.

. 'Ah – Johnson. I'm arranging for someone else to take over your job in the vestibule from Monday week. Shall we say that you'll start in your new post then? Splendid.'

The major felt like answering 'Ay, ay, sir,' he felt so jaunty, but he restrained himself and replied with a calm affirmative. He strode into the house wondering if the rest of the staff knew of his appointment, but no one mentioned it. He hummed a military march under his breath as he arranged his desk, and one of the lady guides said, 'My, major, you are in good spirits today.'

'Indeed I am, indeed I am,' agreed the major.

He was tireless that afternoon, remaining cheerful as the hordes of visitors trooped in and the guides all began to wilt. He directed the hungry towards the orangery and tea with unflagging patience; he counted heads with zeal and accuracy. When he got home that evening he still felt full of energy and decided to wash the car. He left it parked on the gravel outside the bungalow, changed into working trousers and rubber boots, and began to roll the hose out.

From next door the sound of Derek's rotavator ceased. As the major fixed the connection to the tap, the young man appeared in the gateway.

'You haven't a drop of petrol, have you, Major Johnson?' he asked. 'I've run right out – I do want to finish this stretch tonight. This is when one curses because there's no pump in the village.'

'I've some in the garage,' the major said. 'Not much – just enough to fill up my mower once more. That won't last you long. But I've a gallon in the car. I always carry a spare can in the boot. You never know when you'll need it.'

He took the car keys out of his pocket and went round to the back of his car. Bending down, he put the key in the lock.

'That's funny. It isn't locked,' he said, half to himself.

He raised the lid.

Mary was found.

PART THREE

I

DEREK WENT up to the square in his own car to tell the police. It seemed more direct than telephoning to Leckington. They closed the boot of the car before he left, and the major spent the short interval until he returned disconnecting the hose and putting it away again.

Two constables arrived with Derek, and a few minutes later Detective Chief Inspector Coward and Detective Sergeant Davis joined them. They did not take Mary away for some time. First they rigged up tarpaulins to hide the scene from the road; then a police photographer and the doctor came. The press followed, and very quickly a small crowd of spectators gathered on the pavement. Several policemen stood outside the major's bungalow keeping them away.

Chief Inspector Coward went to tell the Formans and to prepare them for the fact that they would have to identify Mary formally, later on. She was removed after an hour, a tiny form on a stretcher covered with a blanket, and a policeman drove Major Johnson's car away to be examined.

Superintendent Harris interviewed Major Johnson himself.

The major could hardly take in what had happened.

'How could she have got there?' he kept saying. 'Why wasn't the boot locked? I always lock it.'

'It wasn't locked? You're sure?' demanded the superintendent.

'Quite sure,' said the major.

'Mr Blunt?' The superintendent turned to Derek.

'I'm not certain – Major Johnson said something about it

being unlocked but I didn't notice, I'm afraid,' said Derek, whose face was as white as the major's. He had been sick in the major's bathroom after they had found Mary. The sight of the child lying there, whey-faced, was one he would never forget. The major had seen many dreadful sights in his life, so he did not vomit, but he felt distinctly queasy.

'You've used the car today?'

'Yes,' said the major. God, how long had he been driving round with that pathetic child lying there? 'I went to Leckington this morning, and to Chorlbury Manor this afternoon – I work there.'

'Your car was here on Thursday night? In the garage?'

'Yes. I used it to go to The Grapes that evening – I usually walk up there at about half-past six or so. There was a thunderstorm that day, so I took the car.'

'I see. And you put it away when you got home?'

'Yes, I did.'

'How long were you in The Grapes?'

'Not long. Twenty minutes, perhaps.'

'And you lock your garage at night, Major Johnson?'

'Always.'

'You locked it on Thursday in spite of the storm?'

It had stopped raining when he got home that night. He remembered standing on the gravel drive sniffing the damp air as he turned the key.

'I know I did,' said the major. 'I'd just collected the car from being serviced and having a new gearbox fitted that morning. Perhaps the garage didn't lock the boot after checking the spare tyre. I'd have probably noticed it sooner if it hadn't been for the storm.'

'You collected it before you gave Mary that lift?'

'Yes – it was ready about half-past eleven. I had lunch in Leckington, at The Feathers.' There was no need to mention Miss Mainwaring; why involve others? The police would soon find out how poor Mary got into his car. 'Could she have opened the boot and climbed in?' he wondered aloud. 'The lid might have dropped shut on her – there wouldn't be much air.'

'I don't think so, sir. There were various bruises on the body. It looks as if she was dead when she was put into your car.'

'Oh dear,' said Major Johnson.

'Yes. A bad business.'

'The poor Formans,' said the major. 'Who could have done it?'

'Done what, Major Johnson?'

'Why, killed her, of course.'

'You think she was murdered?'

'Surely it's the only explanation?' The Mrs Flints were right after all. 'One of these – these child murderers, I suppose, killed her and hid her in my car. But how – when – I just don't understand.'

'We'll know more when the doctor's examined Mary properly,' said Superintendent Harris.

'If you've finished with me, I'll go home,' said Derek. 'It's Cathy's birthday. We've got a baby-sitter coming. We were going out.' He looked at the older men. 'I couldn't eat a thing.'

'You'd better try,' advised the superintendent. 'You don't want your wife brooding too, do you? You'll feel better soon.'

Derek went away.

'Still wet behind the ears,' said Chief Inspector Coward, who had returned from his mission to the Formans while Superintendent Harris was talking to the major. 'Some of our lads have seen worse than that long before they're his age.'

'If you think of anything else – something that might throw light on how anyone could have got at your car – you'll let us know at once, of course,' said the superintendent.

'Certainly,' said Major Johnson.

'And you're not planning to go away, are you?'

'Of course not. I'll be here if you should want me.' What an odd remark.

'We'll want to talk to you when we've examined the car.'

'I shan't be going anywhere,' the major said.

The policeman went away and Major Johnson poured himself a stiff drink. Could someone have put the child's body in his car while it was parked at Chorlbury Manor? It was the

85

only thing he could think of. Once the staff were all in, the courtyard where they parked was deserted. He finished his drink and poured himself another. Then he realised that he had not eaten since midday, so he scrambled some eggs. He was sitting down at the kitchen table, on the point of eating them, when the doorbell rang.

Two men stood on the step. As the major opened the door a flashlight went off in his face. They were reporters, and one of them was the man with a moustache whom he had spoken to in The Grapes the night before.

Major Johnson was very angry.

'Go away,' he said fiercely, and slammed the door,

They rang continuously for some minutes but he did not answer. After a while he heard their footsteps on the gravel. He did not finish his supper.

II

Cathy Blunt was awake early, feeding her baby. She had tried not to disturb Derek, sliding out of bed with as little upheaval as she could manage. Derek gave a grunt and rolled over. She looked down at him, smiling indulgently as she sometimes smiled at Amanda; his hair was tousled and his beard showed dark on his jaw-line. For a while she forgot the terrible discovery of the night before, but when she had finished with the baby and tucked her back into her cot she looked out of the window over the garden, and there, across the dividing hedge, was Major Johnson hoeing his cabbages. At six o'clock in the morning.

Derek put out an arm and gathered her to him as she got back into bed.

'He's out there already,' she said.

'Hmmmm – who is?' mumbled Derek, still almost asleep.

'The Cheshire Cat. In his garden. I suppose he couldn't sleep. Poor old boy.'

'Hum. Yes.' Derek, though very shocked at first, had managed to banish the nightmare to the back of his mind.

'He couldn't have had anything to do with it,' said Cathy.

'Good God, no. He'd scarcely have opened the boot like that if he'd known the kid was there. He had as much of a shock as I did.'

'But how did she get in there?' Cathy persisted. 'Oh, poor Mrs Forman.' And Cathy knew with startling clarity that she, herself, would never live a totally unworried life again, now that she had a little daughter of her own.

'Some crazy maniac,' said Derek. 'Let's forget it now, Cathy. Go to sleep.' He kissed her ear, getting a mouthful of long fair hair as he did so.

But Cathy lay awake, thinking of the child and her parents, and of the odd, repressed man next door who had become so incongruously mixed up with the tragedy.

Later, when they were having breakfast in their sunny kitchen, she said, 'Derek, let's ask Major Johnson to lunch. We've got a chicken – there's plenty of food.'

'Oh, not today, Cathy.'

'Why not? He shouldn't be alone, poor man. He must be feeling awful,' Cathy said.

'No, Cathy. We'll ask him later, when this has all blown over.' Derek finished up his cornflakes. 'I don't want you mixed up in this business, it's bad enough already.'

'Bad enough for the Formans, yes, and the major,' Cathy said.

'I was there, remember, when Mary was found. That's quite enough involvement for us,' said Derek.

Cathy looked at him and her eyes widened.

'You're afraid of being mixed up with a scandal,' she accused. 'Derek, how could you?'

'It isn't good for business,' Derek said.

'But you've just said Major Johnson couldn't possibly have had anything to do with Mary's death. What harm can it do, asking him to lunch?'

'It connects us with him. It might be bad tactics, if it got about,' said Derek. He was on the brink of promotion in his firm, and he did not want to risk blemishing his image.

'Oh, Derek, how can you think like that? When he's been so kind to us!'

'He's rather an odd chap. There's something a bit strange about him,' Derek said. There must be, or how had the body got into the car? Bodies just didn't get into people's cars. Seeking to justify his attitude, Derek suddenly thought with an icy feeling that the major might be suffering from amnesia. He could have killed the child and forgotten all about it. He said so.

'I don't believe it,' Cathy said. Her cheeks were flushed and her eyes were bright with anger. 'He's a nice, shy, harmless old man, and someone's played this terrible trick on him. I'm ashamed of you for thinking like that.'

But the more Derek thought about it, the more sense the idea made. The old man might easily have found out from Mary that she was due at Miss Price's on Thursday evening. He could have waylaid her there. She would have got into his car without a murmur.

'He's not coming to lunch, Cathy, and you're not to talk to him,' Derek said. 'I forbid it.'

Cathy's heart was thumping hard and she felt slightly sick: who was this hostile stranger sitting facing her?

'I shall do as I please,' she said. She was beginning to tremble. 'He's always been sweet to me, and he has lovely old-fashioned good manners.' She got up, went out of the back door, and walked straight down the garden to the bench. She climbed up on it and looked over the hedge.

'Hullo, Major Johnson. Good morning,' she called. 'Isn't it a lovely day?'

And Major Johnson, jolted back from his dark thoughts to the present, looked up from thinning out the lettuces, which was what he was doing now, to her pink, glowing face framed with long fair hair. She looked like an angel appearing over the fence.

'Can you spare some parsley?' Cathy asked.

He gave her some.

But Cathy did not ask him to lunch.

III

The news that Mary had been found dead was given on the radio at nine o'clock, and Miss Mainwaring heard it as she started her leisurely Sunday. Because the Formans were a local family, Leckington had taken the child's disappearance closely to heart, and even Miss Mainwaring felt a personal concern. She looked in her *Observer* for more details before turning to the book reviews, and found a paragraph which disclosed where the body had been found.

Miss Mainwaring's gaze flew to her hydrangea. She was not a nervous woman, but she shuddered. It was some minutes before she felt able to resume her toast and marmalade.

One of Tom's sisters told him the news. She was in her dressing-gown, reading the *News of the World*, with her hair in rollers and cream on her face while Mrs West exclaimed in resigned dismay at her failure to conform to orderly breakfast habits.

'They've found that kid. In some bloke's car, she was,' said Brenda West. 'Look, there's his photo.' And there was a picture of the startled Major Johnson at his front door. 'Rotten bastard,' added Brenda.

'Why rotten bastard?' growled Tom.

'Well, he done her in, didn't he? Must have,' said Brenda.

'Does it say so?' Tom demanded. He snatched the paper from her and read the headlines.

MISSING CHILD FOUND IN MAJOR'S MORRIS, they ran, and the text went on to describe with fair accuracy the circumstances. No details, it added, had yet been released about the cause of death.

'It doesn't say he touched her,' said Tom. He read on, his lips forming the words silently. Then he repeated them aloud.

Major Johnson, a bachelor, said he did not know how the child's body had got into his car.

'Course he said that,' Brenda exclaimed. 'He's not going to admit it, is he?'

'If he killed her, he wouldn't have left her in his car,' said Tom. 'He'd have dumped her.' As they had dumped the bikes.

' 'Spect he was going to, only they found her first,' said Brenda.

'Give your father the paper and get out of my way,' said Mrs West, coming to the table with the teapot.

On Sundays in Wiveldown, since the post office was closed, the papers were collected from a shed in the garden of the senior Flints. The brothers took it in turn, Sunday by Sunday, to fetch them from Leckington and put them out on an old deal table. Whichever brother was then in charge sat there exchanging gossip with his customers as they straggled in. If he got bored, he went away, leaving a tin for the money.

On that Sunday there was no shortage of subject matter, and the village came early for its papers. Most of the papers carried picture's of the major's bungalow, and one showed his car being driven away.

The major was among the first callers. As his firm footsteps sounded on the path the small group clustered round the door of the shed fell silent and stared at him.

'Good morning,' said the major in his clipped voice, and stepped into the shed.

'*Sunday Telegraph*, please,' he said.

Silently the elder Flint folded it and gave it to him. The major always brought the exact price with him; he handed it over and strode off. No other words were said, but when he had gone, the voices broke out.

'Well! Did you see that?'

'Fancy walking in like that, as if nothing had happened!'

'As bold as brass –'

He heard it, as he was meant to, and he squared his shoulders walking on with his usual firm tread. He must expect this for a time; soon the police would discover how Mary had got into his car and things would return to normal.

He walked down the road, back to *Tobruk*, and saw his neighbour Mr Philpot approaching. Major Johnson prepared to greet the other man; Mr Philpot, with great ostentation, crossed the road to the other side and ignored him as they passed.

Mrs Fellowes did not collect her papers until quite late that morning, and when she did the shed was unattended. She had heard the police sirens the evening before and had realised there must be some development in the hunt for Mary, but unlike most of the village she did not know where the child had been found, only what she had heard on the radio news. She walked all the way home before she opened her *Sunday Express* and saw on the front page a picture of Major Johnson's bungalow.

When she rang him up, he had already left for church.

Major Johnson went to church every Sunday morning, so today was no exception. He wore his best grey worsted suit and sat in his usual pew. When he came in, those already in the church nudged each other and stared at him; those who arrived later also stared.

The Reverend Wilson looked round at his flock and saw Major Johnson sitting there. He had assessed the major as a man whose code was Kiplingesque; now he wondered. He took as his text: *Whoso shall offend one of these little ones* and led prayers for Mary and the comfort of her parents, who, being Baptists, were similarly petitioned for in that sister establishment up the road. At the end of the service he stood in the doorway to greet the congregation filing by. He shook Major Johnson's hand firmly when his turn came, and looked hard at his face with his vague blue eyes. The major returned his stare steadily. The vicar was the only person in church that morning who looked at the major and did not turn away.

When the major reached his bungalow a flock of small boys was gathered outside it. At the sight of the major they scattered, but not without a flow of language obscene at any age, but shattering at theirs.

91

IV

A pair of brand new, bright tan boots with a row of ornamental studs across the instep stood on Chief Inspector Coward's desk. He sat before them, staring at them pensively, and Detective Sergeant Davis leaned against a filing cabinet, also in an attitude of meditation.

'A pair of boots like these were nicked from Leckington market last Thursday afternoon,' mused the inspector. 'Two yobbos made a rumpus at the stall, and one of them took the boots while the other chatted up the stallholder.'

'That's right,' agreed Sergeant Davis. He was tired. He had been up most of the night, and so had the inspector, but he felt wrung out, whereas the inspector seemed to be rejuvenated by the extra adrenalin coursing round his system.

'Hm. Well, get out with these to Mordwell, see how they match up. The size may be different, but we should be able to get a pair the same size as the footprint, though it won't be evidence. Anyway, we're not looking for a sex maniac. That'll be some comfort to the parents.' If anything could be. 'I'll go and see them. And I'll call on Major Johnson while I'm there.'

'Do you think he had anything to do with it?'

'No, but it may be hard to substantiate that. Someone else dumped the child in his car, I'm certain. If the fingerprints on those stolen bikes match up with any on his car, we'll have something to go on.'

'And the sherry bottle.'

'Right.'

'It may be difficult to isolate any prints on the car,' said the sergeant. 'The lab boys say it's smothered in them – the garage mechanics and the major himself, probably.'

'There may be something on the boot. The major opened it, so his may be the only ones to show. We'll have to see.'

'They might not have taken well, on a wet surface,' said the sergeant.

'We may get something, if they were at all greasy. No one rubbed the car down. Well, let's get going.'

They separated on their various errands. Detective Sergeant Davis went to Mordwell where he made visual comparisons of the printmarks in the barn with similar ones caused by the boots he took with him, and he sent for a man from the forensic department to make a cast of the one they had found. It had already been photographed. All this took some time.

Chief Inspector Coward found Joe Forman down at the bottom of his garden, where he kept his birds. Even they were silent this morning, not a coo came from a pigeon, not a tweet from a canary. There was no sign of Jean. The Inspector had noticed that all the curtains were drawn in the upstairs windows as he approached the house. At least there were no reporters outside.

'Well, Mr Forman, what sort of night have you had? Rough, eh?' There was really no need to ask, but the conversation had to start somehow.

Joe Forman nodded.

'Been out walking,' he said. 'I didn't go to bed. Jean's asleep now. The doctor gave her something.'

'You should try to get some rest, you know,' said the inspector.

'Would you be able to, in my place?' asked Joe. He looked at the inspector and his manner altered. 'I doubt you've had more than a couple of hours yourself,' he said.

'I'm a father too, Mr Forman,' said Coward. 'This is a bad business, but you can put your mind at rest on one point. She wasn't murdered by any pervert. We've had the preliminary report from the doctor – his full, official one will be through later today – but there was no sexual interference. It looks as if she was killed by a car – she had a head wound, and internal injuries.' He paused. 'The doctor said she died instantaneously – she wouldn't have known about it.'

Joe Forman let out a breath.

'I'd been thinking it must be the major,' he said. 'Though he seemed all right. Used to work up at Walter's. Quiet, though, for an army man. And not married, of course.'

'Is it a crime to stay single?' asked the inspector.

' 'Tisn't natural, is it?' said Joe. 'Makes you wonder.'

The inspector sighed.

'Maybe she wouldn't have him, Mr Forman,' he suggested. 'May not have favoured the roving life.'

'I hadn't thought of that,' admitted Joe.

'He'd have been looked after in the army, in the mess.'

'Hm.' Joe looked abashed. 'I'd been planning to go down there – do him over, maybe.'

'I'd thought you might.' Luckily he had discouraged Major Johnson from calling to offer his condolences.

'He could have done it, though, even so. Run her over, I mean.' Joe's colour rose again.

'Mm. But he's a careful man, the major. Not likely, would you say? Suppose someone borrowed his car?'

'But when?'

'Ah – that's the difficulty. It was locked in its garage all Thursday night, as far as we can tell. But maybe someone dumped Mary in it when it was parked, say at Chorlbury Manor? Someone who'd run over her in their own car.' The doctor had been vague, so far, about the time of death. The car had been standing out in brilliant sunshine at the Manor; it had been hot in the boot.

'If that's it, how will you ever find him?' Joe asked despairingly.

'We'll do everything we can, Mr Forman. Something may turn up,' said the inspector.

'If I could meet the bastard –' Joe clenched his big fists.

'Yes, well –' Chief Inspector Coward turned away. 'We'll find him, if it's possible.'

He got back into his car and drove down to Church Street. The front gate of the major's bungalow was closed, but a group of women, some with prams, stood on the opposite pavement staring at the place and muttering together. Some clutched toddlers by the hand.

In a few succinct words the chief inspector suggested that they would be better employed cooking the Sunday dinner. None of them were churchgoers on their way home; they had simply come to gape.

He spent fifteen minutes with the major checking on where the car had been since Mary disappeared. It had been outside The Grapes for twenty minutes or so, which was long enough for someone passing to stop, open the boot and dump the child, but at the risk of being seen, though few people were out during the storm. Mary's legs were splashed and her sandals caked with mud; her hair was matted and her clothes were damp, though some of the wet had dried off while she had been shut in the car.

'If only I'd looked in the boot before,' the major said. 'Those poor people, the Formans – they'd have known sooner. And you'd have been able to start your search for whoever is responsible earlier, Inspector.'

He looked haggard. Even the neat little clipped moustache seemed to droop.

'But it was lucky I opened it when I did,' the major went on. 'If young Blunt hadn't wanted the petrol I might not have looked in there for several days.'

The policeman knew that the effect of the heat on Mary's body would have made the major wonder what was in his boot before much more time had passed, but he did not say so.

'You may have a little unpleasantness for a day or two, till we get a lead on who may be to blame,' he said. 'There were several women outside just now, and the newspapers haven't helped. Let me know if there's any trouble, and I'll put a man outside.'

'They would think you'd got it in for me, Inspector, if you did that,' said the major wryly.

Chief Inspector Coward went up to The Grapes when he left the major. Both bars were full and the Hursts were busy serving customers who had come from outside the village just to see where the tragedy had happened.

'Major Forman was in here on Thursday evening, I suppose?' asked the chief inspector. 'He comes in most nights, I believe.'

'He does – but not on Thursday. At least, I didn't serve him. I'll see if my wife did,' said Mr Hurst. He went to ask her, returning at once to say that she had not done so.

'But Penny may have – she's our daughter. She was looking after things on Thursday evening early. We went out for the day and didn't get back till after opening time.'

'May I see her, then?'

'Sorry – she isn't here. She's gone off abroad on a camping holiday.'

'She didn't mention serving the major?'

'No. She didn't say that anyone had been in at all. We had our regulars in later, but it was quiet that night because of the weather.'

'Hm. Would she have mentioned Major Johnson, if she'd served him?'

'I don't know. Probably not. But who can tell? She's wrapped up in her own affairs and might have forgotten him. He's not particularly memorable, is he?'

Neither was Crippen.

Chief Inspector Coward went away deep in thought. Every instinct he possessed told him that the major was innocent of all blame, but if there was any connection between the stolen boots, the bicycles, and the major's car, the sooner it was found the better.

V

After she had finished her breakfast, Celia Mainwaring went out into the town to buy a paper which carried a fuller account of how Mary's body had been found than the brief paragraph in the *Observer*. When she saw how some of the newspapers, for want of any other titillating scoop, had exploited the story, she bought several.

After she had read them all and studied the various photographs of Mary, her parents, and the major, not to mention the shots of his bungalow, she looked across at the blue hydrangea. She could not keep it. What had been merely a joke was now a matter for horror. She went to the telephone and rang up Mavis Combe.

Mavis had read the news, like everyone else, but she had not connected Major Johnson with Celia's admirer.

'Of course you can't keep it,' she agreed at once. 'But what can you do with it? Give it to the hospital?'

Celia had not thought about an appropriate means of disposal, but now she knew what must be done.

'I'll give it back to him. I should never have had that lunch with him. He took it as encouragement, obviously.'

'You and your lame dogs, Celia. You'll get yourself into a jam with them one day.'

'It looks as if I've done it now.'

'Not really. I'll take you out there and we'll get rid of it,' said Mavis.

'What – ring the door-bell and hand it to him?'

'Better dump it on the step. We don't want to be clobbered too,' said Mavis, who was five foot eight and had been a physical training instructress before she married.

'No,' Celia agreed.

'I suppose he forgot what he'd done – amnesia – that must be why he left the body in the car,' said Mavis, who had read the case in detail.

'Could be. It's all very nasty. He must be to blame in some way – no smoke without fire and all that,' said Celia. 'Anyway, I don't want to be mixed up with it.' She and Mummy had always kept clear of any unpleasantness.

'We'll go this afternoon,' said Mavis. 'I tell you what, you come over to lunch – Don's got a friend coming but there's plenty. Roast pork. We'll leave the hydrangea in the car and go over when the men have gone out. I'll get Don to fetch you.'

Don was a mild little man who worked in the Midland Bank and as a hobby did brass-rubbing. This took him off for hours at weekends; it was an interest Mavis did not share. They had no children. Donald's friend was a fellow brass-rubber; they were going to Gloucester that afternoon in pursuit of more rubbings for their collections.

They talked about the death of Mary Forman over lunch.

'Major Johnson doesn't seem to have done anything criminal,' said Donald. 'Just owned the car the body was dumped in. It could have happened to anyone. I think you should keep the hydrangea.'

'I can't. I should never have accepted it in the first place,' said Celia. 'I ought to have rung up the shop and made them take it back. There are things one just mustn't do.'

Donald went into the kitchen with a stack of dirty plates and stood there muttering.

'What's that you said, Don?' asked Mavis.

'I said, "The fellow's not likely to rape you," ' Donald repeated, and stood grinning in the kitchen as he put the cutlery to soak before bringing in the gooseberry tart.

'Donald!' cried Mavis. 'You are awful! Take no notice, Celia.'

Donald's friend, however, looked at him with new respect as he brought in the pudding. Old Donald might give that cow of a wife of his hell yet.

VI

Major Johnson looked in the fridge at the chump chop he had bought for his Sunday lunch and felt it was all too much trouble. But he was due at Chorlbury Manor at two o'clock so he must eat something. Without a car, he would have to walk as the buses did not go that way, and he must allow at least half an hour for the journey. If he was lucky someone might bring him back.

He settled for bread and cheese and an apple.

It was hot when he started out at twenty minutes past one, and the thundery, close feeling that had been in the air on Thursday had returned. A lot of cars were parked outside The Grapes. The major walked past and turned to the right. The police had left the school. But in the square, a group of boys with bicycles had gathered. Major Johnson walked by with his eyes fixed straight ahead; he did not recognise any of them, so they might not know him, either. But one did. Next minute, like a swoop of swallows they sped up to him, swerved very close to him as he marched along on the footpath, and rang their bells loudly.

Major Johnson strode on, and the boys circled round, approaching as close as they could. Then they stopped ringing their bells and began to hiss at him through their teeth, not uttering a word. His heart thumped painfully. If they were young soldiers he would be able to quell them at once, but they were not; they were a pack of idle youths with no discipline except that of the mob, and a misconception in their hearts. He wondered what to do. Suddenly, as they swooped round in the road for the sixth time, he stopped abruptly, turned round and glared at them. Anger had made his face go red, but though he was small he was still a figure of authority.

'Stop that!' he bawled at them, and in their surprise two of the boys jammed on their brakes. The front wheels of their bicycles clashed and the riders came off. The other boys had to swerve away to avoid piling up on top of them. While they sorted themselves out, Major Johnson walked on. He calculated that they might lose interest in him when he passed the village boundary, but before this theory was tested a police car came towards them from the Chorlbury direction. Major Johnson heard it slow up after it had passed him, but he did not look round.

He had no more adventures on the way, but by the time he reached the Manor gates he felt very tired. I am getting on a bit, after all, he told himself. Several cars passed him as he trudged up the long drive, bringing the rest of the staff. They slowed when they drew level with him, then went on without stopping. He was puzzled; perhaps everyone thought that as he was so near he might as well end his journey on foot.

But before he reached the forecourt he saw the admiral coming towards him. He wore a dark suit, and for a moment the major thought he was in his naval uniform.

'Ah, Johnson, mm,' said the admiral. 'Just a minute, my dear chap, if you don't mind.' He turned off up a pathway among shrub roses and bushes of spiraea, where it was shady and midges circled in the air. 'I tried to get you on the telephone, but there was no answer.'

'I left early. I had to walk. My car – my car's out of action for a day or two,' said the major.

'Ah yes. Of course. Exactly,' said the admiral. He hunted about for the words to express what he had to say. Damn it, the fellow looked hot, tired, harmless, and what was more, to his experienced eye, utterly reliable. But you never could tell, and he didn't want all the guides walking out, as most of them had threatened to do if the major went on duty. He'd had to deal with some tricky situations in his service life, but never one like this.

'The fact is,' he said, plunging in, 'just till this unfortunate business has blown over, I think it would be wise if you stayed away from the Manor. I'm sure the police will have things sorted out in a day or two, but meanwhile, I'm sure you understand.

The major laughed shortly.

'I understand,' he said. 'And this affects the new job too. You won't want to go ahead with that, as things are.'

'Not just at present, my dear chap. Good of you to see it that way,' said the admiral. It was all going off more smoothly than he could have hoped. 'You hadn't mentioned it to anyone, had you? The new appointment, I mean.'

'No. Not to a soul,' said the major.

'Splendid – splendid. Well, I'll get back – I'm standing in for you, today, as it happens,' he said. 'Follow this path down, why don't you? It comes out lower down the drive. No need to go up to the house.'

No need for you to be seen beside me, you mean, thought the major.

'You'll let me know, admiral, if you want me again,' he said in a steady voice.

'When we need you, not if, Johnson,' said the admiral, quite gentle in his relief, and he walked away.

100

VII

Tom West spent Sunday morning getting in his mother's way. One of his sisters went off on the back of her boy-friend's motor-bike for the day, and the other spread out a length of material all over the living-room floor and proceeded to cut out a dress. Mr West, who was a lorry driver employed by a local cement works, went to his allotment, where he grew prize chysanthe-mums. Tom mooched about, following his mother round the house picking things up and putting them down again, without talking. Finally, exasperated, Mrs West snapped at him.

'Tom, what's eating you? You've got the fidgets properly – sit still, for goodness' sake, or do something useful.'

In the end she settled him down with the potatoes to peel for dinner, while she made a plum pie.

'I'm glad you've got that job,' she said, thumping the pastry on the board with a floury fist before she rolled it out. 'It'll lead on to a better, never fear. Doesn't do to sit about. You were right unlucky, losing that other. You'll get back to the mechanics by and by. P'raps you could go to the tech., evenings.'

'P'raps.' He might at that, if he could ever forget the sight of Mary Forman lying in the road with blood in her mouth. At the moment he felt as if he never wanted to get into a car again. He scratched away at the potatoes. They came from his father's allotment, and though they were large, they still scraped well. His great shock of hair hid his face from his mother's eye.

'You were out in that storm, Thursday,' she said, accusingly. 'Your clothes were soaked. It'll be a wonder if you've not caught a chill.'

'I haven't,' Tom said. He sniffed as if to contradict this, and ran the back of his hand across his nose.

'Use a handkerchief, if you please,' reproved his mother. 'Where were you, then?'

'Where was I when?'

'On Thursday, in that thunderstorm.'

'Oh, out,' said Tom vaguely.

'I know that. Who were you with? You weren't alone.'

'Why d'you ask?' Tom stiffened and turned to face her, the knife still in his hand. 'Someone been asking?'

'No. Why should they?' But it was his mother's turn to look wary. 'I wondered, that's all.'

'I was with a feller you don't know and a couple of birds,' said Tom. He turned back to the sink and dug savagely at an eye in a rather gnarled potato. His mother arranged her sheet of rolled pastry over the pie dish and pressed it down before fluting it expertly all round the edge. She sighed. She knew when Tom was lying.

Tom did not eat much dinner. Afterwards, his sister, her cutting-out done, set the sewing-machine up on the kitchen table. Mrs West took a deck-chair out into the small patch of garden, and Mr West settled down with the paper in the living-room. Soon he would be asleep. Tom slouched out of the house. He had no clear plan in his mind, and without really thinking what he was doing he took the Wiveldown road out of the town.

VIII

A police car took Joe and Jean Forman to the mortuary. Mary looked like a wax doll. There was no visible trace of injury on her; a strand of her fair hair nad been arranged to cover the bruise on her forehead, and her limbs had been straightened. The contusions on her body and the sutures of the pathologist were all concealed from her parents. Joe stood looking at her with tears pouring down his coarse red cheeks; Jean, who had insisted on coming too, was dry-eyed. Detective Sergeant Davis drove them home afterwards and told them enquiries were proceeding in the normal way.

'You mean, you haven't a clue,' said Joe bitterly.

'I wouldn't say that, Mr Forman,' said the sergeant.

By now a thumbprint found on one of the stolen bicycles had been proved to match another on the passenger's door of Major Johnson's car. The stallholder who had lost the boots had given a fair description of the youth who had turned the trestle over, though not such a clear one of his companion. Both were long-haired and dressed in jeans and leather jackets, but the one who upset the boxes of shoes had been a big lad, with large scarred hands and bitten nails, which the stallholder had noticed as they delved about retrieving the scattered goods. However, these attributes were common to a great many youths in Leckington and everywhere else, so finding the right ones would mean quite a search. The police were starting at the homes of known trouble-makers; something might turn up from this.

However, it was no good telling the Formans any of these facts yet; they were all straws in the wind at the moment. He did his best to console them, and then drove down towards *Tobruk*.

Church Street was deserted. It was hot and sultry again, and a Sunday stupor seemed to have descended on the inhabitants of Wiveldown. The police search parties had gone from the area and the visible upheaval connected with Mary's death had disappeared. At the moment there was nothing to stare at.

Major Johnson did not come to the door immediately the sergeant rang the bell. He was about to press it a second time when there came sounds from inside the bungalow and the front door was opened. Major Johnson stood there looking angry; his face was red and his wispy hair was askew.

'Well?' he barked, before he recognised his caller. 'Oh – sergeant – I'm sorry, I was just changing,' he said. 'I went up to Chorlbury Manor as usual today and they sent me home. I'm pitch, it seems. Not to be approached for fear of defilement.'

'I'm very sorry to hear that, sir,' said the sergeant, stepping into the house as the major stood back to let him in. 'Folk are strange when these things happen. You soon find out your friends.'

'You're right, sergeant,' said the major grimly.

'People forget, very quickly,' said the sergeant.

'Maybe. But I shan't,' said Major Johnson. 'Well, what can I do for you, sergeant? More fingerprints? Or samples of blood?'

'No, sir. Nothing like that. Just, if you wouldn't mind, the clothes you were wearing on Thursday when you gave Mary a lift.'

Major Johnson looked at him for a long moment.

'Very well, sergeant,' he said heavily. 'You'd better come along and take your pick.'

He led the other man through the hall and into his bedroom. The sergeant looked around, poker-faced; he had surprises every day and he had one now. He might have been in an army barrack, or even a prison cell. A narrow divan bed stood against one wall; it was covered with a chocolate-coloured woven spread. There was linoleum on the floor and one small, black mat beside the bed. A white-painted chest in one corner had a small shaving mirror standing on it, and the major's hair-brush with a comb neatly stuck into the bristles. There was also a large clothes brush. A single upright chair stood below the window. Beside the major's bed was a plain white table with a gardening encyclopaedia on it, and a lamp with a white plastic shade and a wooden base. There were no pictures; no concessions to comfort. A fitted cupboard was built into a recess, and this the major opened, to reveal his clothes neatly hanging, with his shoes side by side below.

Major Johnson took out a tweed jacket and sorted through several pairs of trousers.

'I had on grey flannels. These, I think,' he said.

'Shoes?' asked Sergeant Davis.

'This pair. The ones I'm wearing.'

'Shirt?'

'Washed,' said the major crisply. 'I wash my shirt every night and hang it in the bathroom to dry. And my socks the same. I have a few better shirts which I send to the laundry along with sheets and towels.'

'You don't go to the launderette, then?'

'I do not,' said the major austerely. He had thought of it, but could not face the mob inside, even though he saw that many of the patrons were male. He had been far too long insulated from this sort of enterprise. He sat on the bed, unlaced his shoes and took them off. The sergeant, who felt embarrassed because the major was somehow displaying enormous dignity throughout the encounter, bent and picked them up. They were warm from the major's feet.

'I was about to change my shoes in any case,' the major said. He had worn his best grey worsted suit to go to the Manor; now he was dressed in twill trousers and a sports shirt, with a cravat at the neck. He looked neat, if heated, and could never have been mistaken for anything other than a retired soldier. He took a pair of navy-blue canvas shoes from the cupboard and put them on, tying the laces firmly.

'Anything else, sergeant?' he asked, before closing the cupboard.

'No, sir. That will be all, thank you,' said Davis. He put the garments into various polythene bags he had brought with him, and then packed them in a leather holdall. 'We'll let you have them back as soon as we can.'

The major led him to the front door and opened it. Both men looked down in surprise. There, on the step, was a large blue hydrangea in a pot.

IX

'He went quite pale. Looked awful – he was flushed and over-heated-looking when I got there.'

Detective Sergeant Davis was sitting in the chief inspector's office describing his visit to *Tobruk*.

'Did he explain?' asked Chief Inspector Coward.

'Didn't want to. I dragged it out of him. Seems he'd sent it to a lady, and she didn't want it. There was a note with it.

He read it and crumpled it up. Went scarlet in the face again.'

'Bad for the arteries.'

'Mm.'

'Who was she?'

'He wouldn't say. Very chivalrous, the major.'

'You didn't see this female?'

'No. I hadn't heard a car, either, while I was there. The major's bedroom is at the back – overlooks the garden. Grim, it is, too.' He described it.

'Poor Major Johnson. He lacks a woman's tender touch, obviously,' said the inspector. 'Maybe the hydrangea was an attempt to secure it. Shouldn't be too hard to trace her – get on to the florists. Can't be all that many pot plants bought at this time of year. With luck there'll be a record of the major as purchaser. She may be a Wiveldown lady – hence you hearing no car. She might have come on foot.'

'Conspicuous, eh? Carrying a plant.'

'Mean way to act,' said the inspector. 'Now, let's get round to see some of our bad lads. Find out where they all were on Thursday.'

'Before we do that, sir, there's one other thing I noticed after I'd left the major,' said Davis. 'May not mean much, but I've a hunch it could.'

X

The newspapers had wrung the last possible drop of human interest out of Welbeck Crescent and its residents while Mary was still missing. Now, until her funeral could give that angle a fillip, they were concentrating on the police enquiries. So when Joe and Jean Forman returned from their trip to the mortuary on Sunday afternoon there were no reporters round their gate. After Sergeant Davis had gone, Joe said he was going to see Ted Smith.

106

'You be all right?' he asked his wife.

She nodded.

'I'll be off then.'

Joe left her. He could not think of a word to say to her nor any comfort that he might give her. Their tragedy should have drawn them together, he felt obscurely, but instead it seemed as though what had been a small crack between them had turned into a vast gulf. As for himself, he had to turn somewhere in this nightmare; a cup of tea and a chat with Ted and Betty might help.

Jean went up to her bedroom when he had gone and sat in front of her mirror. A pale, drawn face looked back at her. What would happen now? What was the point of anything? She gazed round the pretty room with its white fitments picked out in gilt paint. Joe had done them for her. She had made the padded headboard for the bed herself, following the instructions in a magazine. It was a room anyone would be proud of, not just a housewife on a council estate.

Automatically she brushed her hair, fair like Mary's but helped with a brightening rinse, and put new lipstick on. Then, at last, she went into Mary's room. It was very tidy. Her mother-in-law had been in and put away the clothes Mary had left out after changing into her Brownie uniform. Dully, Jean looked round. A stuffed bear wearing a gingham dress and apron lay on the bed; there was a row of china animals on the window-sill. Mary's yellow dressing-gown hung on the door. The furniture in here was painted apricot colour, and a white acrilan rug lay on the patterned carpet beside the bed. It was a charming room for a little girl. Jean stared at it. Then she went to the cupboard, opened it, and looked inside. Mary's dresses hung there, fresh and crisp. She gazed round the room once more. Something was wrong, not accounted for, but she could not think what it was.

She went downstairs again and into the kitchen, where she put the kettle on for want of any other occupation. She felt completely numb, as if she were dead herself.

When a tap came at the back door she jumped.

The handle turned and it opened slowly.

'Who is it?' she called out sharply.

'It's only me, Jean,' said a man's voice, and the door opened fully.

'I saw Joe leave, so I came round,' he said. 'There, love.'

He put his arms out to her, and the woman who had been able to get no comfort from her husband collapsed into this other embrace and wept.

After a long time Tony Miller said, 'I'd better go. Someone may have seen me come in, or Joe may come back.'

Jean said, 'It doesn't really matter now, does it? The point's gone. It was Mary, really.'

Tony stared at her.

'You mean you'd leave Joe now?'

'Why not?' said Jean.

Tony looked at her face, blotched with tears; she no longer had the ability of a young girl to weep without looking ugly. Did he want her after all? He'd tried to persuade her, often enough, but wasn't part of the excitement the feeling that she'd never really leave her family – that she would always be just out of reach?

'You can't decide anything now, while you're so upset,' he told her. 'There's plenty of time. I'll still be around.'

But would he? He'd have to make his mind up quick.

When he had gone, Jean wondered for a while if she would leave Joe and go off with Tony. He was young – too young maybe; vigorous, and on their stolen Wednesday afternoons in the back of his car, very exciting; but she was five years older. He was doing well, it was true; he earned much more than Joe already and he was ambitious; he would go far. But in a year or two he might tire of her and want someone younger.

She sat there turning it all over in her mind and reaching no conclusion. Then she realised what had worried her in Mary's room. The police had not mentioned finding her satchel, yet she had taken it with her, the day she disappeared.

'How's Jean taking it?' asked Ted.

'Seems kind of stunned,' said Joe. 'Hasn't said much at all.' How could he say that Jean and he had not been able to communicate? 'She looked so pitiful, Ted, did Mary. Sort of shrunken, like a little doll.'

'Pity you had to see her.'

'I had to, Ted. I couldn't have believed it, without.'

'Heather's pretty upset,' said Ted. 'Betty's taken her black-berrying – not that they're really ripe yet – but to keep her busy, like. If they'd been together on Thursday it wouldn't have happened.'

'Might have been both of them, not just Mary,' said Joe. 'You can't tell.'

'Those chaps – those madmen who lure little girls – they don't usually try it when there's two,' said Ted. He lit his pipe and puffed at it slowly. It was a good thing Joe had come down; he'd something to tell him, and it was better said when Jean couldn't hear it.

'It may not have happened like that,' said Joe. 'She may not have been lured. They think she was run over.'

'Yes – but not here – out of the village. She must have been taken away first.' Of course she'd been enticed away; it was the only explanation, but Ted knew if it were Heather, he wouldn't be able to accept it either, he'd reject the thought. No punishment was too bad for a man who hurt a little kid; it was all very well to say such criminals were sick: what about the victim?

'She'd know Major Johnson. Wouldn't think of him as a stranger,' said Ted.

'Of course she knew him. He gave her a lift that afternoon.'

'Maybe he arranged to meet her again, later. Perhaps he said he'd pick her up after she'd been to Miss Price.'

Joe stared.

'Why should he?'

'Bit odd, maybe. Taken with her, very likely. Anyone would

be.' Ted didn't want to be too blunt, all at once. 'Solitary sort of individual, isn't he? Doesn't have any friends. Says very little if you meet him in the pub.'

'I've always got on with him,' Joe said. 'He was liked at Walter's.'

'That's another thing. Why did he leave there? Too grand, was he, for factory work? Better up at the Manor with the admiral and the lady guides?'

'He only sells tickets at the door,' said Joe. 'Jean and I took Mary along there a while back, and he spoke to us real nice.'

'And why wouldn't he? You'd got your pretty little girl with you and he wanted to be friendly.'

'What are you trying to say, Ted?' Joe asked. 'I don't get your meaning.'

'I'm saying that I don't think Major Johnson has told the police al¹ he did on Thursday,' said Ted. 'I think he met Mary in the evening and took her for a drive.'

'But it said in the papers he was in The Grapes.'

'I know. Who told them that, though? The major, that's my guess. The Hursts don't remember seeing him that night. I asked them,' Ted said. 'In any case he'd have had time to kill Mary and put her in the boot, and go in for a beer afterwards.'

Joe shivered.

'Or he may have dumped her somewhere, and fetched her later.'

'But why? Why should he want to hurt her.'

'Because he's kinky – a nut. That's why.'

'But she was run over, they say.'

'Yes,' said Ted. 'Very likely. Afterwards.' Ted knocked his pipe out on the hearth, making a nasty mess of tobacco bits. Jean would hate a thing like that, thought Joe, irrelevantly. 'I saw the major's car, later on Thursday night, Joe. When I was walking back from Miss Price's after looking for Mary, it passed me. A dark green Morris 1300, it is.' The whole of Britain knew that, and the registration number. 'I checked today that no one else living down his end of Church Street has a car like that. Philpot, the butcher, in the big house, has a Jaguar and his

110

wife has a mini, and that young couple have got a Triumph Herald – one with a soft top.'

'But, Ted,' Joe insisted. 'She wasn't interfered with. The police wouldn't say that if it wasn't true.'

'Might have looked, though,' said Ted. 'We'll let the police find out, eh? I'll ring them, shall I?'

Joe was silent, and Ted waited patiently. Of course he'd resist the truth; who wouldn't?

'Very well, Ted. Yes, ring them,' said Joe at last.

XII

Major Johnson stared at the hydrangea. It was on the table in his sitting-room, where he had put it after the sergeant had gone. He sat in one of his twin armchairs and he felt completely stunned. He was tired after his long walk to and from the Manor. When he drew near to the village on his return he had made a detour to avoid the square, in case the boys with their bicycles were still there, but he had felt this to be an act of cowardice. He was completely innocent of any implication in the death of Mary, so he had nothing to fear. His clothes had been taken because the police must eliminate all possibilities, so that was not a matter for concern. But he had never before felt at first hand the effect of rumour. His army career had followed a prescribed path; there had always been the next duty to carry out, the next promotion to deserve, finally the respect due to his seniority, until at last the gulf in age between him and the other officers of similar and even senior rank had been too much to ignore. He had done well, he knew, rising from band-boy to major; he had served his country loyally in many lands, not in the forefront of the battle, but in just as vital a way, behind the scenes. Now he deserved peace, at least. He had not foreseen the loneliness retirement would bring, and now, just as it seemed that he would conquer even that, this tragedy had happened.

He had not told the police about his visit to Mrs Fellowes' house because it was not connected in any way with Mary's disappearance, in his view. It was the same reasoning that made him refuse to divulge the name of the lady to whom he had given the hydrangea. There was no justification for involving either of them in this sorry business. Mary could not have been anywhere near Mrs Fellowes' house on Thursday evening; Miss Price lived on the other side of the village. She must have been put in his car while it was at the Manor, and it was sheer chance that it was his car which was used, not someone else's.

His fault lay in leaving the boot unlocked.

If he had still been in the army there would have been a colonel, and after him a brigadier, to go to now with this load of worry. However much younger than him they were, they would be duty-bound to help him. As things were, there was no one. He thought of the vicar, and dismissed him at once; he was kind, true, but vague; and Sunday was his busy day. He'd got at least one more service to take. No, time would be the remedy; in time the real culprit would be found.

He faced what the return of the hydrangea meant. Miss Mainwaring had read the Sunday papers and she shared the reaction of the women who had watched him walk back from church, and the louts on their bicycles with their hissing. And those women at the Manor, the cultured grey-haired ladies with their rigid vowels, they were no different. Even the admiral was the same.

He would sweat it out. In a few days the truth, whatever it was, would be known, and these same people who had shunned him would forget. But he would not. How could he?

He stood up and looked at his bugle, brightly shining above the mantelpiece. Then he turned round, picked up the hydrangea and marched with it out into the garden where he hurled it from him across the lawn. The pot hit a stone in the rockery and was smashed; the plant lay on the grass surrounded by the scattered peat in which its roots had lain.

A moment before, Cathy Blunt had come down her own garden path with a large slice of home-made coffee cake on a

112

plate. She meant to stand on the bench and call to Major Johnson, if he were in sight. Derek was out, fetching the petrol he had intended to borrow the day before, so she'd seized her chance. He'd have to go at least to Leckington to find a pump open on Sunday. She had been horrified at what the papers said, and more, what they implied, when as far as she could see the major was simply the victim of circumstance. But now, standing on the bench, she saw him fling the plant across the lawn and then stand, staring at the wreckage, hands on hips and grey wispy hair on end.

What sane man would do a thing like that, she asked herself, feeling slightly sick. She clambered quietly down and took her piece of cake back to the house.

XIII

By the time Chorlbury Manor closed at half-past five, Ruth Fellowes had spent a wretched afternoon. She had been in one of the cars which had slowed at the sight of Major Johnson and then sped past him in the drive.

'What a nerve – fancy showing his face here,' Madge Fazackerley had said.

'What? What on earth do you mean?' Ruth was genuinely bewildered. 'Do stop for him, Madge.'

'He must have killed that child,' said Madge.

'What – ' Ruth was incredulous.

'Of course, he did. It's obvious.'

'It's not at all.' Ruth was almost speechless.

'Ruth, be your age. How did the body get into his car if he wasn't involved?'

'I should think that's proof that he wasn't,' Ruth snapped, recovering. 'You'd hardly open the boot of a car in front of witnesses if you'd put a body in it.'

'Amnesia,' Madge said. 'He did it in a fit of insanity and forgot about it.' She stopped the car with a squeal of brakes and backed into the spot the major usually chose. 'We're damned lucky he didn't pick one of us, but I suppose his tastes must run to little girls.' With that she got out of the car.

Ruth did too, more slowly because it was a very small car and she was folded up to fit into it.

'Major Johnson is a thoroughly nice man, Madge. He wouldn't hurt anyone, much less a child. You must stop talking like that,' she said.

'I shall refuse to stay if he comes on duty,' was all Madge answered.

Ruth soon found that this was the view of almost all the guides. She saw the admiral walk down to intercept the major, and then return alone. Later, they were so busy that she suspected some of the visitors had come to the house merely to see the major; several people asked where he was, and some pressmen called to take shots of him at his post. Tomorrow's headlines were tailor-made by his absence, Ruth thought bitterly.

After the house closed the guides had their first chance to discuss the drama, and they proceeded to tear his character to shreds.

'Always thought him odd – far too quiet,' said one.

'These lone men – very sinister,' said another.

Ruth exploded with anger.

'It's no crime not to marry – why should he, if he doesn't want to? He must have had plenty of chances.'

'And why didn't he take them, then?'

'Because he didn't want to end up in a prison perhaps, like some of you,' said Ruth, her temper snapping. 'Suppose this had happened to one of your husbands, or sons? It could have, just as easily as it has to Major Johnson? What would you say then?' She glared at them. For once her height was an asset. Silly bitches; she pitied their husbands.

'But our husbands and sons don't pick up little girls, Ruth,' said Madge.

'If they see them hitch-hiking, and they know who they are, I'm sure they do, for fear the child really does get picked up by someone who might harm her,' Ruth said. 'Madge, are you taking me home? I'm in a hurry.'

Madge shrugged at the others. If Ruth was going to get in a state she was better removed. She went out to her car, and the other guides followed her and Ruth. Admiral Bruce watched them go; he had heard the excited female voices and Ruth's spirited defence of Major Johnson but had basely stayed out of the argument. The Manor closed on Mondays; with luck the whole thing would be sorted out by Tuesday, when it re-opened.

Ruth could not bring herself to speak to Madge throughout the journey back to Wiveldown; when they reached the village she asked to be dropped in the square, where she got out of the car with a curt word of thanks. She had not been so angry for years.

When Madge drove off she walked rapidly towards Church Street and hurried down it to the major's bungalow. Derek Blunt in his Triumph Herald passed her and waved. At least the major had pleasant neighbours, thought Ruth; the Philpots were reasonable people, too.

A youth was sauntering down the road ahead of her, eating crisps from a bag. He was tall and thin, dressed in shabby jeans, and with a great bush of curly hair that stood out round his head in a fuzz. He walked slowly, looking at the houses as he passed, and then he paused opposite *Tobruk* and stood staring at it. As Ruth drew nearer he became aware of her and turned away, walking off at a faster pace than before. Ruth did not recognise him. She opened Major Johnson's gate, walked up the short gravel drive, and rang the bell.

There was no answer.

She rang a second time. He must have got back hours ago. Had he walked all the way? It was a long walk on a hot day. She peered in at the front window but could see no one in the sitting-room.

Ruth walked round the side of the house and into the garden. Across the lawn, beyond the vegetable beds, Major Johnson was standing over a bonfire. Ruth went towards him. He had not seen her. With half her mind she noticed how very neat

115

the garden was; the lawn was closely mown and there seemed to be not a single weed, but just at the edge of the grass, where the rockery began, there were a few bits of peat or potting soil spoiling the general neatness, and a fragment of broken flower-pot. Ruth picked it up.

The bonfire was not going well. There were hedge trimmings on it, and something blue: what looked like a large hydrangea in its prime. Major Johnson was stabbing at it fiercely with a fork and there was a reek of paraffin in the air.

She did not want to startle him.

'Major Johnson,' she called.

She had to call his name a second time before he turned and looked at her. His face had a wild, ravaged look, and his sparse hair was bedraggled. Sweat poured off his forehead.

Ruth was not a particularly imaginative woman, but she was fifty-five years old and she had seen a lot of life. Even so, today's reaction at the Manor had astounded her. If so-called cultured women, many of whom had led relatively sheltered lives, could behave in such a way, so could other people. Major Johnson had, no doubt, discovered this.

'You look very tired,' she said. She was too shy to call him by his first name, though she knew it from the newspapers. 'This is awful for you. Do leave the fire and come indoors. Let me make you some tea, or have you any brandy?'

He hesitated, and she took the fork from him, as she would have with a child. Then, silently, he let her lead him back towards the bungalow.

XIV

None of the Sunday motorists who passed Tom stopped at the appeal of his upturned thumb and he walked all the way to Wiveldown. He did not know where Major Johnson lived, but he could find the bungalow; the village wasn't large. There might even, he thought in a wilder moment, be a cordon of police all round. In the square a group of boys were wheeling and swooping about on bicycles; they were like a flock of birds, communicating by some means of thought transference; suddenly they coalesced and shot off down a side turning. When they had gone, Tom mooched over to the post office and stared in the window. Among fly-blown notices about pensions and television licences there lurked a few faded sweet cartons; it was a drab and dingy exhibition. He ambled on and gazed at tins of peaches and pears in the grocer's window. If he asked where Major Johnson lived he would draw attention to himself.

He would walk all round the village. In that way he would, eventually, come upon the place – what was it called, an odd name, some old battle – *Tobruk*, that was it.

He spent the afternoon wandering about. Wiveldown's cricket club had cancelled their match because all the men had been out searching for Mary; instead of the small crowd usually to be found on their field at weekends there were just five small boys who had set up a wicket at the side of the pitch and were playing a game amongst themselves. A woman with a basset hound on a lead was walking round the edge. It was hot and close; most folk were at home, sleeping off the Sunday lunch or working in their gardens; few had gone out in the car for the day, for the village still felt stunned by what had happened and had withdrawn behind its ramparts.

Tom found himself in the road where the accident had happened. He forced himself to saunter nonchalantly past where the car had been parked, casting a glance at the cottage standing high above the road. This was not the major's house. The tarmac surface of the road had melted slightly in the sun and was tacky under his feet; there was no trace of Thursday's accident. The air felt heavy; he could hear bees humming about and smell a heady smell, the scent of flowers in Ruth's garden where roses hung above the road. He could see now where Mary had come from; there was a gap in the hedge filled by a stile. Tom climbed over it and wandered across the field. It took him some time to find his way out, for he would not go through the next one which was full of cattle, but after circling about

117

and climbing various gates and fences he came to another road. It was, he saw, the Leckington road, which he had walked along some time before. On the far side there was a wooden gate, the paint on it chipped and green with mould, and beyond it a mass of shrubs. He could make out a house beyond them; it looked deserted. The major did not live in that one.

He walked back into the village again and turned right in the square. The boys with their bicycles were back, standing astride the machines, talking in a stationary group. As he walked along a solitary policeman in a car drove towards him. The man was not in uniform but the car had a sign and a blue lamp over the windscreen, neither operating. Tom stared straight past it and the driver ignored him. Tom went on, and soon came to a turning on the left with a sign saying *Welbeck Crescent*. Trim semi-detached houses stretched away on either side of it; Tom's feet turned up that way without his mind ordering them. Number Thirty-three was halfway up on the left. The curtains were pulled across the lower windows and there were blinds drawn upstairs. Marigolds and dahlias blazed in the garden, far too gaudy for a house of death. The grandmother lived in this street too, but Tom couldn't remember where. In some of the gardens, children were playing. Normally, the bigger ones played on the wide grass verges or even in the road, but today only the teenagers were outside their own bounds. A group of girls whispered together across the road from Number Thirty-Three. They kept glancing at the Formans' house. Two women talked over a hedge. Several men were washing their cars. It looked peaceful, but Tom felt menace in the air. He came to the end of the Crescent at last and found himself back in the other road.

He saw a close of bungalows opposite to him, and walked round that, peering at all the names above the doors or on the gateposts, but none was called *Tobruk*. Suddenly, when he was almost at the church, he came upon another bungalow; it crouched, squat, between a large brick-built house covered in virginia creeper, and a smaller, white-painted one which was set back from the road at the end of an approach drive. Over the bungalow's door hung a sign with the name *Tobruk* upon it. Tom's heart thumped so hard that he could not look properly at the place now that he had found it. He hurried on to the church at the end of the road and went into a shady corner of the churchyard, under a yew, to decide his next action. An old man in a cassock with white hair and a beaked nose came out of the church while he stood there biting his nails. Tom panicked. He vaulted over the low stone wall and cowered in the grass on the far side, but the Reverend Wilson had not seen him.

After a while Tom pulled himself together and went back up the road. There was no one in sight now. As he drew level with the major's bungalow a maroon Triumph Herald with the hood down came out of the drive beside it and turned up towards the square.

The major's bungalow looked tranquil. There was no policeman to be seen, much less a cordon of them. The garage doors were closed and so were all the windows at the front. Maybe the major was out. Tom walked on. It had been silly to come. He couldn't expect to meet Major Johnson face to face, and that was what he really wanted, to see what sort of a geezer he was.

He went back to the cricket field and sat on the ground for a bit, watching the kids. They took no notice of him. He'd bought some crisps and a Bounty Bar on his way out of Leckington, and he ate the chocolate while he sat there. Then he got up and wandered back again down Church Street, eating the crisps. Still there was no sign of life at the major's bungalow. Tom glanced over his shoulder and saw a woman coming down the road towards him. She was tall and grey-haired, walking fast. He went on towards the church again, and when he glanced round once more the woman had vanished.

XV

As he drove away with the major's clothes, Detective Sergeant Davis saw Tom West walking down the road. He did not know

119

the boy, although his face was vaguely familiar. Some instinct, the one that regarded checking the major's clothes as a mere formality, prompted him to stop alongside the boys with their bicycles clustered in the square. They all made as if to ride away at once but he called out sharply.

'Wait a minute, there.'

'We ain't causing no obstruction,' said one lad aggressively.

'I didn't say you were,' said the sergeant mildly. 'Name, please.'

The boy glowered, but eventually gave his name. The sergeant asked the others their names, round the group, and sulkily they answered. He wrote nothing down.

'Two bicycles were stolen from a farm near here last Thursday and dumped down Lammas Lane. Know anything about it, any of you?'

'No. We all got bikes, ain't we? What we go nicking them for, then?' said one boy.

A reasonable answer.

'That a mate of yours just went down Church Street?' asked the sergeant.

'Never seen him before.'

'Not a Wiveldown boy, then?'

Heads were shaken all round.

'Don't live here,' said a small, tow-haired boy with freckles.

'Right, then.'

The sergeant left them to their cycling. There was a lot to be said for the village bobby, he thought ruefully. He'd been one himself, once, and had known every family in his area and its potential for good or ill. The boys were speaking the truth about the stranger in their midst; if he had been a village boy they would have denied seeing him at all.

As he drove into Leckington and passed the boarded-up garage property, soon to be demolished, where Tom had worked, recollection came to him. That was where he had seen the boy in the past.

Chief Inspector Coward listened in silence to the sergeant's report of this chance meeting.

120

'Just a hunch, eh?' he said when it was over.

'The boy was alone. He had a great mop of curly hair. So did one of the lads involved in lifting those boots in the market. He doesn't belong in Wiveldown so why was he there?'

'Visiting his auntie.'

'Maybe.'

'Hm. Well, put someone to finding out who he is, and when you've done that we'll get on out after some of our other friends.'

He was still waiting for Sergeant Davis to return from arranging this when Ted Smith telephoned and told him about seeing Major Johnson's car late on Thursday night.

XVI

Major Johnson, letting himself be shepherded into the bungalow by Mrs Fellowes, felt like a small boy in the clutch of a firm schoolmistress. He surrendered briefly to her authority, but once they were inside his own sitting-room self-consciousness returned. As Ruth took in the austere room, Major Johnson felt the obligations of a host crowd in upon him. Neither had spoken since Ruth's one sentence in the garden.

'Mrs Fellowes – '

'Some brandy. You need some.'

Both spoke together, but it was Ruth who continued. She saw that the major, who had been very red in the face, was now pale; she went on in the commanding manner which she had cultivated so hard over the years that now it was second nature.

'Sit down. Tell me where you keep the brandy.' He must have some.

'In there.'

He pointed to a carved mahogany sideboard. She found the bottle and a glass and poured him a stiff tot. He gulped it down and his colour began to return.

121

'Don't talk,' Ruth instructed. She refilled his glass, and then sat down facing him. The hairy upholstery of the rather uncomfortable chair prickled her legs through her tights.

Major Johnson sat in obedient silence, alternately sipping the brandy and breathing gustily. He studied his shoes, the canvas ones he had put on under the sergeant's gaze. They were covered in dust from the bonfire. He had taken off his cravat and his shirt was open at the neck. Wisps of wiry grey hair were visible. I'm not respectable, he thought dully, but he could not muster the strength to put matters right. After a bit he spoke.

'I'm sorry – how rude – you must excuse – '

Ruth cut him short.

'I saw what happened at the Manor. I couldn't get here any sooner. It was disgraceful,' she said.

The major grimaced.

'People believe what they want to believe. The papers only told the truth. My car was used. How, I don't know.'

'Have the police any idea who did it?' Ruth asked. 'They can't let this happen to you.'

'They've taken away my clothes for some form of test,' said Major Johnson. 'They must eliminate me, I suppose, before they look for someone else.'

'Could someone have taken the car without your knowledge?'

'I don't think so. I always lock it, even in the garage, here.'

But on that one day he hadn't checked that the boot was locked, when he brought the car back from Leckington. When he took Mrs Fellowes home in the thunderstorm, had he locked the car? He couldn't remember doing so. But it had been just where he'd left it, outside her house, when he went home. He rubbed a hand across his forehead, leaving a smear of ash.

'Inspector Coward will get to the bottom of it. I'm sure he doesn't think I'm to blame,' said the major.

Maybe, but you'll be crucified first, thought Ruth.

'I wonder how long it will take him?' she said.

'The laboratory work all takes time. It's not twenty-four hours, after all, since the child was found. I expect it will all be sorted out in time for the inquest.' Major Johnson was beginning to feel better. 'Won't you have a drink, Mrs Fellowes? You see, I'm quite myself again now. You prescribed excellent medicine.' He managed a smile.

Ruth, who had seen that the interior of the sideboard contained a good assortment of bottles, asked for a gin and tonic. He would be bound to keep her company by having another drink himself, and a mild alcoholic haze was, she felt, his best defence against despair.

'You'd like some ice,' he said, pouring her drink. 'I'll have a quick wash, if you'll forgive me, and then get it.'

'You wash – I'll find the ice,' said Ruth, standing up.

'Oh – how kind – ' he said. He looked a little put out, but Ruth, towering over him, smiled in her firm, cooking-class manner and he did not argue.

She went into the kitchen, which was very small but spick and span. In the refrigerator she saw one chump chop, half a pound of margarine with a small piece missing from one end, a half-full milk bottle, four eggs and two tomatoes. She took out the ice tray, and opened a cupboard seeking a bowl. She found the shelves sparsely loaded with a tea service such as might be bought at a knockdown price in a bargain department, and some dinner plates which did not match. She put the ice in the sugar bowl. Impelled partly by curiosity and partly by compassion, she opened a couple of drawers in the sink fitment. There was a full set of stainless steel cutlery which looked as if it had never been used. One knife, fork, and spoon were set apart in a separate section of a fitted drawer, apparently for daily use.

She closed the cupboard and the drawers, filled the ice tray with water and replaced it. A washing-up mop and a dish-cloth were tidily stowed at the side of the sink, the cloth on a hook and the mop between two small clips. It was all so neat, and it was utterly bleak.

She had time to take in the full austerity of the major's sitting-room before he returned. She saw the bugle, gleaming, over the tiled mantelpiece, the square of drab, sand-coloured carpet, the single picture, a print of Windsor Castle. There were no books, no ornaments, not even a cushion except the upholstered seats of the two armchairs. At least there was a television set.

At this point in her appraisal of the room, Major Johnson returned. He wore a clean shirt and his regimental tie. A triangle of spotless handkerchief protruded from his blazer pocket and his precious strands of hair were neatly flattened. He looked his normal self, but in her mind's eye Ruth still saw the sweating, angry man stoking the bonfire.

XVII

Mrs Brewis had her hair in rollers and was watching television on Sunday afternoon when the police called. She knew at once that the firm knock on the door meant trouble; useless to pretend to be out, for they would have seen the flickering screen through the window. She shuffled into the hall in shabby bedroom slippers; her varicose veins ached.

She knew Chief Inspector Coward.

'Well?' she demanded truculently, but her heart sank. What had Roger been up to now? He'd disappeared, and that was proof enough that he'd something to run away from. It must be serious, as the inspector was here himself.

"Evening, Mrs Brewis. Mind if we come in?' said the inspector. 'This is Detective Sergeant Davis. You haven't met each other before.'

This tea-party treatment did not suit Mrs Brewis. She glared at the two men as she grudgingly opened the door wide and stood back. Better to have them in than the neighbours gaping while they stood on the step. As it was, their car was outside for everyone to see. She led the way into the living-room and turned the sound down on the television. There was a smell of boiled cabbage in the air, and a tap could be heard dripping in the kitchen.

'Your boy home, Mrs Brewis?' asked the inspector. He

could tell from the atmosphere that there was no one else in the house. 'We'd like a word with him.'

'He's out just now,' said Mrs Brewis.

'When do you expect him back? Will he be long?'

'Don't know, do I? Can't tell with boys. Depends.'

'Where's he gone, then? Out with his mates? Let's see, who's he running round with now? Young Jeff Cardew's gone down for a couple of years, hasn't he? Left your boy a bit lonely, hasn't it?'

'Roger's not been in no trouble for a long time,' said Mrs Brewis.

'Glad to hear it,' said the inspector.

He got up and went over to the doorway that led into the kitchen while Sergeant Davis took up the questioning.

'Been in work this week, has he?'

'Casual like,' said Mrs Brewis. They could not prove otherwise. 'Odd days.'

'Where was that, then? Down on the building? Done a bit of labouring, hasn't he?'

'Odd jobs, he's been at,' said Mrs Brewis.

'Got his card stamped, has he? Hope he's given you a few quid, then. Tough, your life, isn't it?' said Coward, from the doorway. 'You still cleaning at the bank?'

'No. I got a job at the supermarket. Better money. And I do part-time at the laundry, too.' She recovered some spirit and added, 'You want to keep up to date.'

'Ah. That's good. Because you need a bit, don't you, with Roger not bringing any in?'

'Who said he wasn't bringing none in?'

'He's not been home for some time, has he?' Coward remarked, coming away from the kitchen. Mrs Brewis was not houseproud, and he could see on the drainer, upside down, one cup, one saucer, and a dinner plate. 'Where is he, then?'

'I don't know. I told you.'

'When did you last see him? Now, come on, Mrs Brewis. I can ask next door, you know. Some of your neighbours will know when he was at home. Wouldn't you rather tell me yourself? They'll be nosey enough as it is.'

'He's not done wrong. I'm sure he hasn't,' Mrs Brewis blustered, but her defiance was giving way to fright, and her voice shook slightly.

'When did you last see him?' repeated the inspector patiently.

'Thursday morning. He was here Thursday morning.'

'I see. And when did he leave? Went to work, did he?'

'No, not Thursday. He went out about eleven. Didn't say where he was going.'

'You weren't at work yourself?'

'I was back. Have to be at the shop at seven-thirty. It opens at half-eight. I go down to the laundry after dinner.'

'Hm. Two lads caused an upset in the market on Thursday. Turned a stall over and nicked a pair of boots. Your Roger didn't come home on Thursday with a new pair of boots?'

'Never saw him.'

The inspector nodded at Sergeant Davis, who got up and left the room. They heard his feet heavily ascending the stairs.

'What size feet has your Roger? Eights? Nines? Big chap, isn't he?'

'He takes nines.' Useless to hide it; there'd be some old sneakers or something of Roger's upstairs. 'You've got no warrant,' she added.

'Don't need one, when you're being so helpful,' said the inspector. 'He's left home, has he?'

She shrugged.

'He's done it before,' she said. 'He'll be back.' And then, recovering some of her fire, 'why do you have to pick on Roger? You don't know as it was him in the market.'

'No, but it could have been, from the description. It's his style, too.'

'Huh – what's a description?' she said scornfully.

'Two bicycles were pinched later, down at Mordwell. They were ditched near Wiveldown.'

'Wiveldown? That's where that kid – ' Mrs Brewis did not end the sentence.

'Yes. That's where Mary Forman lived.'

126

Mrs Brewis said nothing.

'Roger's left home before to escape trouble,' said Coward. It was a statement not requiring an answer. The boy had been mixed up with a gang who had done several breaking and entering jobs, and disappeared, two years before. They'd been found in Brighton.

'He's not a vicious boy,' said Mrs Brewis in a faint voice.

'No?' said the inspector. He looked up as the sergeant returned. 'Well, that's all for the present. Send him round to see me, if he comes back, won't you?'

She could not speak, and she made no attempt to go with the two men to the door.

'Well?' said the inspector when they were back in their car.

'Pair of sneakers upstairs. Couldn't see the size so I took them.' He patted his pocket. 'And a pair of winkle-pickers – very old – out of date now. Not good for size-matching. She was scared, all right. Worn out, too.'

'She's had a bad time of it. The boy's father was inside more than he was out. Nothing violent – mostly petty thieving. Then he got in with a mob who pulled a bank job. One of them had a gun. Her old man got five years and when he came out he left her flat – and the boy. We'll put out a call for him.'

'And Major Johnson?'

'It's odd about Thursday night. I wonder where he was?' mused the inspector. 'I still don't think he's got anything to do with this, but we'll have to ask him. Perhaps he was tucked up in bed with whoever he gave the hydrangea to. He seems anxious to hide her identity.' It seemed unlikely, somehow. 'We'll talk to him tomorrow. We'll have the full report on the car by then. He won't run away.'

'No, poor bastard,' said Sergeant Davis. He thought complacently of his own comfortable semi-detached house on the outskirts of Leckington, and his plump, pretty wife. With luck he'd be home before dark.

XVIII

Ruth was constantly being cast by life in the role of authority to whom others turned in time of crisis, so it was second nature to her now to take command. Therefore, when she and Major Johnson had had their drinks, she asked him what he had eaten for lunch. Very little, seemed to be the answer.

She could cook that chop for him, but would he eat it if she did?

'Have you any tins of meat?' she asked him.

'No. Why?' He looked surprised. 'I shop from day to day. It makes for a little routine, don't you see?'

She did: a framework for his empty day.

'You must have something now – I'll just run round to Cathy Blunt and see what I can borrow. You go down your garden and dig up some potatoes and pick some beans. I'll cook a meal for both of us. I only had a snatched lunch today.' It was true. She had been so upset at the newspaper accounts of how Mary had been found that she had not bothered to cook anything.

'Oh no – ' he began, but she interrupted.

'I've known Cathy for years. She's sure to have something. I'll repay her in kind. And I'm hungry, even if you aren't. I won't listen to any protests.' She stood by the door. 'Now, have you a basket? Something to put the vegetables in? You can help by slicing the beans.'

She saw him start meekly on his way down the garden and then she went next door. The roar of the rotavator filled the air as Derek churned the soil. Ruth opened the front door and let herself in, calling to Cathy, whom she thought would be busy with the baby now.

In fact Cathy was just ready to put Amanda down in her cot; she came to the top of the stairs holding the small bundle against her.

'Ruth! Is something wrong?' She came quickly down the stairs.

'It's Major Johnson,' said Ruth, and saw a guarded look come over Cathy's face. 'You know him – you said you'd always found him a pleasant neighbour.'

'I've always thought him a dear old boy,' Cathy said, and then wondered if that was tactful, since he and Ruth must be much of an age. 'But now –'

'You don't think he had anything to do with this business, surely, Cathy? You've got more sense.'

'I didn't – but – ' Cathy hesitated, and then came out with the story of the hydrangea.

'Would Major Johnson be likely to buy himself a pot plant for the house?' Ruth demanded. 'Use your brains, my dear. Have you been inside that house? It's about as comfortable as a prison cell. He tried to give the plant to someone and they sent it back.' For the major, realising he must explain his odd behaviour, had admitted as much.

'Oh dear,' said Cathy. 'How awful!' She looked at Ruth in dismay. 'And I'm no better,' she added, and confessed about the coffee cake. 'Derek doesn't want me to talk to him,' she finished.

'Well, you must decide what to do about that yourself,' said Ruth. 'What you can do now is lend me a tin of something – stewed steak for choice, or mince.' She explained her intentions.

'Oh, Ruth, you are good,' said Cathy.

'I'm not. I'm bossy and interfering,' said Ruth. 'But I can't go home and leave him like that, miserable and unfed. I'm good at feeding people. It's what I'm trained to do.'

'I've got some mince – there may be something better, I'll look,' said Cathy. 'Hold Amanda while I do. Do you want anything else? Rice or something?'

'No – he's got potatoes, and bread.' Ruth had looked in the bread bin.

Cathy handed the baby over and went into the kitchen. Ruth followed, holding the child against her sensible courtelle shoulder.

'Imagine what other people are capable of, Cathy, if even you, a normal kind-hearted girl, could think as you did,' she

129

said. 'He's having a terrible time.' She told Cathy what had happened at the Manor.

'Here's some steak. It's not bad,' said Cathy. 'I'll keep an eye on him over the fence, Ruth – chat him up. I'll be friendly – give him my love or something, poor old boy. I feel rather ashamed.'

Ruth hurried back to the bungalow. She had been longer than she expected because of her talk with Cathy so Major Johnson should have finished his errand in the garden. She found him standing on the front step talking to a youth in jeans with a shock of curly hair. The boy turned as she approached, said something to the major, and hurried past her.

'Who was that?' asked Ruth.

'I've no idea. One of the village boys, I suppose. He wanted me to find him some sort of job for an hour or two – washing the car, he said.' The major laughed, a mirthless bray.

'What an odd time to call. So late,' said Ruth. She had seen a boy in the road earlier; it must be the same one.

'He seemed a nice lad. Very polite. Doesn't do to judge by appearances, does it?'

PART FOUR

I

CHIEF INSPECTOR COWARD always got a great sense of satisfaction when he had accumulated enough facts to draw in a net. When a case was unresolved his mind kept coming back to it and fretting over what was known; if he was convinced of how a crime had been committed but lacked evidence to prove it, he experienced a sense of personal failure.

He sat in his office on Monday morning with the reports of the Forman case spread out around him and listened to the latest information, as related by Detective Sergeant Davis.

'Shall I go and see this Miss Mainwaring?' asked the sergeant at the conclusion. Only one of Leckington's three florists had delivered a blue hydrangea at the weekend; an assistant remembered it was ordered by a small elderly man with a moustache, who had given no name.

'I don't think so. Not just now. We'll go and see the major. He's got to tell us a few things we haven't found out for ourselves.' He picked a paper up from his desk. 'Here's the report on the car. See what you think about that.'

'Right, sir.'

'Traced that boy yet? The pump attendant?'

'Got a constable on to it now, sir. Should have something soon.'

'Hm. Seen the papers?'

'Yes. Done us well, haven't they?'

Most of the morning papers carried a photograph of Roger Brewis taken two years before when he went to Borstal for six months. In it, his hair was cut short. *Wanted for questioning in connection with mystery death of child*, said one paper, and went on to reveal that the police believed Roger Brewis might have been in Wiveldown when Mary died.

'Someone may bother to tell us they've seen him,' said the Inspector.

Detective Sergeant Davis went back to his own desk with the report on the car. There were traces of Mary's blood on the gear lever, but nothing on the bumper or the tyres. However, it had rained so hard the night she was killed, and the major had driven so much since then, that any signs might have disappeared. There was some distinctive mud in the boot, and on the child's sandals, but none that matched in the interior of the car. There were numerous unidentified fingerprints besides the major's, and other details.

They were on their way to Wiveldown when a call came through from headquarters. One of the two milkmen who served the village of Wiveldown and who did not come on Sundays, had called at a house named *The Hollies* and found the pint he delivered on Saturday still on the step. He'd rung and knocked, but got no answer from the householder, a Mrs Pollock. It seemed he seldom saw her, but there were usually signs of life such as a tea towel on the line when he arrived. A Panda car was on its way.

'We'll go too,' said Chief Inspector Coward.

They left the car in the road outside *The Hollies* and walked up the overgrown path. The weeds were lush after the storm, and under the trees the air smelled dank. There was still thunder about, and it had rained again in the night.

'What a place,' said Davis. 'Looks uninhabited.'

As they approached the front door a tabby cat bolted round the side of the house and shot between the inspector's legs. No one answered when they rang; the doors were all locked and the windows fast. There was a cat-flap in the back door. The unclaimed pint of milk stood in a box on the back step with a slate on top of the bottle to protect it from the birds.

In the end Sergeant Davis broke open the kitchen window and climbed through on to the draining board. He saw Mary's satchel hanging on a chair beside the table before he saw the old lady.

Chief Inspector Coward left Sergeant Davis to wait for the doctor and some more men and went himself into the village to find out what he could.

The post office was the obvious place to call, and as the milkman had telephoned from the box outside it, the two Mrs Flints were eagerly waiting for the next development. They were peering from their windows, their knitting in their hands but the needles still. When the police car stopped they were stabbed into the balls of wool, one tangerine, one lime, and both ladies came round from behind the counter.

'Poor Mrs Pollock. She's dead, of course,' said the elder Mrs Flint.

'I'm afraid so,' said Chief Inspector Coward.

'Oh dear, we'll all be murdered in our beds next,' said Deirdre Flint with relish.

'Who mentioned murder?' asked the inspector.

'Well, first little innocent Mary, and now this – '

'As far as I know, no one has said anything about murder at all,' said Coward. He stepped into the post office. 'There will be an inquest on Mary tomorrow, and that will determine the cause of her death. Mrs Pollock probably died of old age – heart, I should think.' The fact of Mary's satchel being in the house must be kept undisclosed at present. 'Did she come into the village at all?'

'Not often – led a life like a proper hermit,' said Marilyn Flint. 'Wouldn't have anyone to the house. Even Mr Duckett – he's the grocer – just put her order down on the step.'

'She'd come in for her pension now and then,' said Deirdre. 'About once a month. And she'd send off a letter to Australia at the same time.'

'Australia, eh?'

'That's where her family is.'

'I suppose you don't happen to have noticed the address?' asked the inspector innocently. It was doubtless engraved on their hearts.

133

'Well, funny you should ask,' said Marilyn. 'I did, as a matter of fact. Her writing was a bit shaky, see, and I'd print it out again sometimes, to make sure it arrived. She always wrote to just the son – Dennis Pollock's his name. I'll write it down for you. In Queensland, it is.' She bustled away back behind the counter, massive buttocks wagging under the yellow crimplene. Chief Inspector Coward repressed a shudder; it was hard to stay impartial.

'When did Mrs Pollock last come in to draw her pension?' he asked.

'Oh – a few days back – let's see, which day was it? Thursday, that's right, and next day Mary'd disappeared.'

'It was quite a walk for her.'

'There's a path from the square goes along to the main road. It's shorter. She always came that way.'

The path had been well combed during the search for Mary. And had no one called at *The Hollies* then? Someone was in for trouble.

'Thank you, Mrs Flint,' said Coward.

'Oh, not at all, inspector. Any time.' Marilyn bared her gums at him and saw him to the door, and when he had gone two customers who had not liked to enter while he was inside hastened to find out why he had come.

The doctor had arrived at *The Hollies* when he got back there, and agreed that the old lady's death looked at first glance as if it was natural.

'Find anything else besides the satchel connected with Mary?'

'No, but we're only just starting,' said Sergeant Davis. 'There are some letters in the sideboard in the hall, from Australia. Oh, and the old lady's purse, with some money in it, and her pension book.'

'Check the lot for prints. And Mary's satchel too. We can't be sure she brought it here herself. Now I'll get down to the major.'

Major Johnson was cleaning the windows of the bungalow, using a small pair of folding steps to give him the extra inches he needed. When the car stopped outside his gate and Chief

Inspector Coward got out, he got slowly down from the steps and laid his leather across the top of the bucket.

'Good morning, sir. I'd like a word, if you don't mind,' said Coward.

'Come in, inspector,' said Major Johnson. He led the way into the sitting-room and sat down silently, indicating the other easy chair to the policeman.

'No more trouble with sightseers, I hope, major,' said the inspector genially. The major looked a wreck, as if he had not slept for a week. He was as neatly turned out as ever, but his face was haggard and the policeman saw that his hands were shaking. He clasped them in front of him in an effort to steady them.

'I had some horrible letters,' said Major Johnson. 'Dozens of them. I haven't read them all. They were – vile.'

'That happens, sir, I'm afraid.'

'The papers said nothing that wasn't true. It was what they implied – useless to sue,' said the major. 'It was just the way it was slanted.'

'Very unpleasant, sir. The sooner we get to the bottom of it, the better.'

'What about that boy? The one mentioned in the paper today, Roger Brewis. Do you think he had anything to do with it?'

'We aren't sure, sir. We think he was concerned in the theft of some bicycles we found dumped near here. There may be a link.' It was too soon to tell the major that Roger's prints were in his car. 'Now, sir, information has come to me that you were out late on Thursday night. Your car was seen turning in at your gate sometime after eleven o'clock. That doesn't tally with what you told us.'

'I didn't specify a time, did I?' asked the major.

'You went to The Grapes, left about six forty-five, and put your car straight in the garage, I think you said. I'd better tell you that neither Mr or Mrs Hurst remembers serving you that night.'

'But – ' Major Johnson passed a hand across his forehead.

He had a headache, at least he supposed that was what the pain in his head was; it was unlike anything he'd experienced before. 'The daughter – it was the daughter served – the daughter, it was,' he said confusedly. 'She'll tell you.' And so would Mrs Fellowes if she were asked, but she had gone to Tenby today to stay with a friend, she must have left by now. Anyway, why should she be drawn into this sordid affair?

'She's gone on holiday, the girl. Pity neither of the parents saw you.'

'Yes. I suppose it is.'

'You went somewhere else after that, didn't you, Major Johnson?' Suddenly the inspector's voice had grown stern. 'Did you, or did you not, return home at about eleven o'clock?'

'I did,' said the major in a dull voice.

'Where had you been?'

'Dining with a friend.'

'And who was that?'

'A lady,' said the major. 'I prefer not to give her name.'

'Would that be Miss Celia Mainwaring?' asked the inspector, and saw Major Johnson go even paler than before.

'No – certainly not,' he snapped. 'Keep her out of it. She has nothing to do with any of this.' How had they discovered he knew Miss Mainwaring?

'The other lady's name, sir, then.'

'I don't see why I should tell you, inspector. Look at what's happened to me, because of this unfortunate affair. My name and reputation bandied about in the papers. Do you wonder that I want to protect my friends?'

'Major Johnson, I must point out to you that you could make a lot of trouble for yourself by keeping silent,' said the inspector. 'If you say where you were, and the lady confirms it, we shall know you weren't in the village when Mary was killed.' Could the old boy really be having a giddy sex life on the side, Coward wondered. It didn't seem likely, but he'd had bigger surprises before.

'It was just a friend, and I didn't run Mary over on the way,' said Major Johnson. He tried to speak calmly but he felt thoroughly mulish by now. Let the police damn well find out who'd killed the child; he knew he hadn't done it. British justice and the British police were supposed to be so wonderful – let them show a bit of initiative now.

'We found a trace of blood in your car from the little girl,' said Coward. 'And there was a hair on your jacket we identified as hers.'

'I gave her a lift in the afternoon. You know that. She had a plaster on her leg – a sticking-plaster thing. Maybe the blood came from there.'

There had been an elastoplast strip on Mary's knee when she was found.

'And the hair?'

Major Johnson shrugged.

'I suppose children do lose hairs like older people. She'd longish hair. If one got caught on the seat it might have transferred itself on to my coat.'

'Major Johnson, you could have run the child over and put her in the boot yourself,' said Coward.

'Are you accusing me?'

'Not yet. I'm just saying that on the facts we've got it could have happened.'

'At least you're not implying that I murdered her,' said the major.

'Mary was run over. She had a blow on the head and internal injuries. The car must have passed right over her body.'

'Why don't you tell the papers that?'

'They'll know in good time.'

The major was silent.

'You've no more to tell me?'

'Nothing that is the least relevant.'

'You're being very foolish, Major Johnson. You're withholding evidence that might help us to find the person responsible. And it's in your own interests to prove that you weren't that person.'

'I'm not going to tell you where I was that night, Chief Inspector.'

137

'Well, then, perhaps you'll tell me how long you spent with this lady?' Coward decided to try another tack.

'Oh – three hours – a bit more, perhaps.'

'So someone could have put the child's body in the car during that time without your knowledge?'

'Yes – yes, I suppose so,' the major agreed. 'But it seems very unlikely.'

'Why?'

There was no answer.

'You mean the car was parked outside the lady's house?'

Still no answer.

'I wish you would tell me, sir,' said Coward. He knew that this thrust was the right one.

'Well, I won't,' said the major. 'You can damn well find out for yourself, if it's so important.'

After the inspector had gone, Major Johnson sat without moving for some time. Why had he been so stubborn? It was silly, really. Mrs Fellowes would be the first to rebuke him. But the police couldn't seriously think he had anything to do with Mary's death. Someone knocking her down with another car and passing Ruth's cottage that night could have switched her body across but it was most unlikely to have happened then. Hardly any traffic went that way. No, the transfer must have happened some other time and Chorlbury Manor was the likeliest place. It was random chance that had chosen his car. He would keep that kindly woman out of all this.

She'd made them a delicious meal, the night before, out of the steak. He'd go up to Duckett's himself, later today, to replace it. Mrs Fellowes had said she couldn't do this herself for a day or two as she had this long-standing arrangement to stay with a friend in Wales. She wouldn't let him see her home. He was tired, and she was quite used to walking about the village. She was much too old and ugly and enormous to fear attack, she said, and laughed.

He felt forlorn when she had gone, but it had not occurred to him to contradict her description of herself.

As he sat in his chair reviewing the chain of events he

remembered something. While he and and Mrs Fellowes had been so comfortably enjoying their evening in her cottage on Thursday, there had been a sound from outside. A car horn had hooted, one sharp, short blast.

II

Tony Miller sat in his bedroom at The Rising Sun reading the *Daily Mirror*. On the front page was a picture of Roger Brewis and a paragraph asking anyone who had seen him to communicate with the police. Believed to have been in the tragedy village, said the paper.

Last Thursday night, after the Wives' Club meeting, Jean Forman had slipped away promptly and hurried up the street to where Tony's car was parked in an unlit patch. He'd whipped her away, out of the village, to a quiet spot for a bit of a cuddle. There wasn't time for much, before Joe got back, but any week now Tony'd grown confident she'd ditch the club and spend the whole evening with him. It would be weeks before Joe found out she wasn't with the other women – if he ever did. They'd be able to keep it up till one or other of them tired of it. But there was something about Jean that was different from women he'd been mixed up with before; that was why he hung around in spite of her prevarication, and why he'd gone to see her after reading about the kid. A terrible thing, that. But not his fault, nor Jean's.

And now there was this picture of the youth.

After leaving Jean near the turning to Welbeck Crescent but not close enough to be observed by nosey neighbours, Tony had gone on to Bletchford, where he knew a widow always glad to see him. He'd met a lad hitching, and had picked him up. He'd left him at an all-night transport café where he'd be sure to get another lift.

Tony did not want to get mixed up with the police. He'd just been home for the weekend; his wife spent the whole week counting the days till Friday when he got back from his week's selling, and the weekend lamenting that Monday must come so soon. The life suited Tony; home comforts every weekend and freedom while he travelled in his area. There was no lack of company, but until Jean he'd never felt tempted to become deeply involved. She'd no idea, naturally, that he was married. They'd met when he went into the shop where she worked, with his samples; he was new to the district then. He'd seen her later, walking away from the shop on Wednesday, early closing day, and he'd stopped to talk to her. They'd ended up having a bite together in a pub. So it had all begun; she was restless, tied to a dull, unambitious man whose efforts did not meet her aspirations, ripe for an adventure. The prospect of spending the rest of her life in Welbeck Crescent was at this moment filling her with despair; she wanted more than that for Mary and herself. Tony was seriously wondering if he would offer to give it to her.

Now this.

He'd have to tell the police about Roger. The boy had seemed just a normal, loutish youth; they'd told crude jokes to one another as they drove along. He'd not seemed vicious. But if he'd been mixed up with poor little Mary's death, that altered things. Not that Tony had met Mary. Jean hadn't allowed it, for she was bringing the kid up primly. But he'd seen her in the distance. He'd no kids, himself.

He'd not ring up, though; they'd hear him from the back. He didn't want the landlord knowing all about it. He'd call round at the police station.

He felt better having made the decision. Once this was done with he'd pull out his hooks and find another base for working this territory. Give him time to think a bit, and Jean a chance to get over what had happened.

III

Joe had gone to work that morning. He couldn't stop at home; he'd nothing to say to Jean, and there was nothing he could do for Mary, not ever, any more. He felt better when he got to the factory. His mates were surprised to see him, but once they'd got over the first embarrassment their sympathy was comforting. Many of them knew Mary, who'd been to works social occasions with him. As he carried out his duties Joe began to feel some sort of life returning to him; but how he'd get through to Jean, well, that was another thing.

He'd left her going through Mary's clothes. She'd asked the police where Mary's satchel was, and they'd said it hadn't been found. They were going to look for it; finding it might throw some light on what had happened. Now she was parcelling up bundles of sweaters and dresses to give to charity. It seemed as if she wanted to blot out Mary utterly, already.

He'd tried, during the night as she lay in bed with her back to him, to talk to her. He'd wanted to say that they could have another child one day, when all this was behind them. She was only thirty-five, after all. But she wouldn't listen and she'd drawn away from him as if his touch was poison. She'd get over it, he told himself. She wasn't going to the shop. With Mary dead her prime motive for work had gone; now there were no piano lessons to pay for, no need to go on putting money away for the bicycle Mary would have had on her birthday; no hurry for the next instalment on the lounge suite. She didn't seem to mind being left alone, in fact she appeared eager for him to leave.

Nothing had happened as a consequence of Ted telling the police that he had seen the major's car late on Thursday. Joe didn't like it; he didn't think the major was a bad bloke. But Ted might be right. You couldn't tell. More would come out at the inquest, probably. That was what Inspector Coward said.

Meanwhile the days must be got through. And the nights.

IV

The paper boy was back. Major Johnson found his *Daily Express* stuck into the gate. He was relieved to be spared the

141

mascaraed stares of the Mesdames Flint. He took it in and read all about Roger Brewis on the front page. It made him feel better.

Soon he would go up to Duckett's to buy the replacement tin of steak for Cathy, but it was too early yet to call on her. He cleaned the bungalow from one end to the other, putting polish on his bedroom lino with a rag tied round a mop as he had done when he was a young soldier. He rubbed it up the same way. Then he got his laundry ready; the man called on Tuesdays. Routine, that was the thing; if you stuck to that you couldn't go far wrong. He'd clean the windows, then walk up to the shop. He wouldn't go to Leckington today. Maybe he'd have his car back by tomorrow, but if not, he might go in by bus. Or would the inquest be held then? He would have to go to that, presumably. He'd like to confront Miss Mainwaring in the library. If he didn't do it quickly, he never would.

A black lump seemed to fill his chest when he thought of Miss Mainwaring. She, who had seemed so clever and good, was no better than the anonymous letter writers in her condemnation of him. Even when the real offender had been brought to justice he would never be able to forget her action.

He was thinking like this, rubbing away with the leather at the windows, when Chief Inspector Coward called.

It was some time after the inspector had gone before he could return to his task. Surely the police couldn't seriously think he'd had anything to do with it? Only a madman, having committed such a crime, would keep the body and then expose it in front of a witness. But surely only someone insane would kill a little girl?

But she hadn't been murdered.

Or had she, and her body been put on the ground and run over, as a blind?

That was a new thought, and the major didn't care for it. Wouldn't the police know? Scientific tests would show it, wouldn't they?

And what had the inspector meant when, as a parting remark, he had said, 'Remember what you said to the constable.

142

Very significant, that. "Mary *was* a nice little girl," you said. Not "Mary *is* a nice little girl." As if you knew her to be dead.'

'But good heavens – ' Major Johnson had blustered. 'Anyone might say that, in those circumstances.'

'Well, you did, didn't you?' the inspector had said, and departed.

How could those lads who'd stolen the bicycles be involved? Maybe they'd seen something. The car that had hooted while he was with Mrs Fellowes – whose was that? But Mary couldn't have been killed in Lammas Lane – she'd no reason to be there. It wasn't on her way home from Miss Price. And no one had taken his car; it was exactly where he had left it when he came out of Ruth's house.

But had it been locked? He couldn't be sure. He always did lock it; routine again; but he had failed to check that the boot was locked so his efficiency must have been slipping.

His brain reeled from sleeplessness and going round in circles. He'd finished the windows. He'd go up the village now, buy the meat, and take it round to Cathy.

Monday was never peak morning in Duckett's Stores. Most housewives were busy with their washing and cleaning up their homes after the weekend. Mr Duckett was alone in his shop when Major Johnson entered. He greeted the major in the normal way and they conducted their transactions calmly. Major Johnson bought two tins of steak, one to have as a spare himself, and a few other items. He still did not feel like cooking, but he had promised Mrs Fellowes to eat properly, so he bought some fish fingers too. As he was paying, a woman came into the shop.

"Morning, Mr Duckett,' she said, and stood rigid in a corner of the shop by the deep freeze, as far away from Major Johnson as she could put herself.

"Morning, Mrs Brown,' said Mr Duckett, accepting the major's money.

'Heard about Mrs Pollock, have you? Deirdre Flint just mentioned it. Awful, isn't it? There'll be a third, sure to be. Who next?'

'Very sad about Mrs Pollock, yes,' said Mr Duckett. 'But she was nearly ninety. Liable to go at any time, I reckon.'

'Took her groceries up there, didn't you?'

'Aye. But I hardly ever saw her. She left the money for me, and a list.'

'She came to the post office for her pension. In there Thursday, she was. Same as Mary. Whoever killed that poor child may have lured her to her death too.' Mrs Brown cast a baleful look at Major Johnson as she said this.

Mr Duckett was counting out the major's change.

'She wasn't killed, was she, Mrs Brown?' he said, looking for a halfpenny piece at the back of the till. 'No one's said that. Old age, you'll find. There you are, major.'

'Thank you, Mr Duckett.'

'Thank you, sir.' Poor bastard, he looked a wreck this morning, thought Mr Duckett, who was keeping an open mind. He'd always found the major very pleasant.

'Well, the nerve!' exclaimed Mrs Brown as the shop door fell to behind the major. 'Fancy coming out as bold as brass.'

Mr Duckett did not answer. He had no intention of gossiping about his customers.

'What can I get you, Mrs Brown?' he asked.

'Half of butter, please – New Zealand. And a pound of granulated,' said Mrs Brown, to be going on with. 'That man, I mean! Major Johnson. After what he's done! You'd think he wouldn't show his face. When are the police going to arrest him? That's what I'd like to know.'

'We don't know that he did anything, Mrs Brown,' said Mr Duckett. 'And the next thing?'

'A bag of flour – self-raising. And some Daz. He must have done it. Stands to reason. And walking about without a care, planning the next if you ask me.'

'It's all circumstantial, Mrs Brown,' said Mr Duckett. 'Just his car was concerned. That's all we know.'

'No smoke without a fire is what I always say,' said Mrs Brown.

Another woman entered the shop then and she turned to her. 'Don't you, Lily?' she enquired.

'Don't I what, love?'

Mrs Brown put forth her theory, and between her statements Mr Duckett got her somehow through her list of needs. Major Johnson might be as innocent of any crime as little Mary was herself, he thought, yet these women would never be convinced.

Major Johnson walked back down the street in a particularly upright, soldierly manner, his back a ramrod. He kept his eyes fixed to the front, but he met no one except the vicar, who had heard about Mrs Pollock and was on his way to *The Hollies*, not that it would do the old lady any good. The Reverend Wilson drove past the major without stopping; he must talk to the man sometime soon, he reminded himself, but there was no hurry. He had seen the headlines in the Sunday papers, but he had not read them yet in detail; he saved them until Monday afternoons.

Cathy felt so guilty because of the bad thoughts she had allowed herself to have about the major that she greeted him almost too effusively when he offered her the tin of steak across the hedge. Poor Cheshire Cat, his grin was rather weak this morning. She invited him round to admire Derek's rotavating. A devastated area lay before them where once there had been long grass laced with tall white daisies.

'He got too keen and swept away my annual bed,' said Cathy. 'I'd got it as a temporary thing, until we'd laid some flower-beds out properly, like yours.'

'You'd quite a show, hadn't you? Larkspur and marigolds. I've admired them over the hedge,' said Major Johnson.

Cathy made him stay to coffee. He did look awful, pale and with dark sleepless marks under his eyes.

'You must come to dinner soon,' she said. 'We'll have a celebration. Derek's going to be promoted.'

'Ah – splendid.'

'I'll ask Ruth too.'

'Ruth?'

'You know Ruth. Ruth Fellowes.' Surely he knew her name; they'd mentioned her before.

But the major had forgotten it.

V

Tony Miller had a long session at Leckington police station. Detective Sergeant Davis was still at *The Hollies* investigating Mrs Pollock's last hours when he got there, and Chief Inspector Coward was with Major Johnson; in their absence the sergeant who took his statement was punctilious, checking times and everything else to the last detail. He typed up Tony's statement, got him to read and sign it, and was about to let him go when the inspector came back.

He took Tony straight into his office and went through it all again. No one was interested in why he was going to Bletchford, so his widow's name was not disclosed, which was just as well in case Jean, or even his wife, heard about her. He was sure the boy was the one in the photograph, and when asked to describe him and his clothes, mentioned the boots he was wearing. He had noticed them particularly because they were very muddy; they also looked new.

'Cleaned your car out yet?' asked the chief inspector.

'No, I haven't – very slack of me,' Tony said, looking surprised.

'Good. Let's have a look at it, then. Outside, is it?'

'Yes. In your yard. I thought I'd be safe there from getting a ticket,' said Tony with a grin.

Chief Inspector Coward hustled him down the stairs and into the yard where the grey Ford Capri was parked.

'This it?'

'Yes.' Tony unlocked the driver's door and leaned across to open the passenger's. He kept a lot of samples in the car and was meticulous about locking it up. 'It is in a mess. I usually wash it on a Sunday, but I was back home with the wife, and that.' He grinned again, man to man, at Coward.

'I'm very glad you didn't clean it,' Coward said. He was peering down at the floor in front of the passenger's seat, his bulky body wedged in the doorway. 'There's quite a bit of mud here. I'd like you to leave your car with me for a couple of hours. It's very important to trace that boy and prove he was in Wiveldown. We'll need to test this mud, and there may be some other things.'

'Yes, I see that. He didn't do poor little Mary in, did he?'

'We don't know what happened yet,' said Coward.

'I thought it must be that old man – the one with the car,' said Tony.

'Anyone been in your car since you picked the boy up?' asked Coward, not commenting on this remark.

'I took the wife down to the local on Sunday. Just a mile or so.'

'Ah – handed her in, did you? Opened the door for her, I mean?'

Tony thought.

'Yes, I did,' he agreed, and laughed. 'How d'you know? I've been married five years.'

'You're away from home a lot. Courting habits sometimes last when that's the case,' said Coward. 'Means she won't have superimposed her prints over the boy's. We may find something.'

'Keep the car as long as you like,' said Tony. He reached over to lift a case off the rear seat. 'I can make a few calls in Leckington, so I won't be wasting my time.'

'Right. Thanks, Mr Miller,' said Coward. 'We must hope whoever picked the boy up after you did will come forward too. But we'll find him, anyway.'

When Tony left the chief inspector was busy with a pair of tweezers and a plastic bag picking up grains of dried mud from the floor of the car. Tony couldn't see how the mud would help, but if it would collar whoever bashed that poor kid of Jean's, then good luck to the inspector. He walked off filled with mixed emotions; the whole thing might blow up and his involvement with Jean be discovered. Well, it couldn't be helped.

Shaking his head, he took his bag into the Star and Garter. He was parched.

VI

Constable Forrest, new to the force, had tracked down Tom West. It had taken him all the morning and part of the afternoon, but he'd done it, and the report of his endeavours, neatly typed, rested on Chief Inspector Coward's desk alongside one from the lab. that confirmed mud found on Mary's sandals and in the boot of Major Johnson's car as identical with that in Tony Miller's Capri. And Tony, when he fetched the car, had agreed that the boots Roger was wearing were the same as a pair in the chief inspector's office. Rather unusual ones, heavy for the time of year, Tony had thought when he saw them, but these lads had to follow the latest trends.

Chief Inspector Coward gave thanks for an observant and positive witness. He asked Tony not to leave the district without letting him know, and they parted.

Mary's prints had been found on Mrs Pollock's purse; no one else's, except the old lady's. Mary's fingerprints had also been found in various places at *The Hollies*.

'So now we can guess where Mary went after she left Miss Price,' said Coward. 'Mrs Pollock must have dropped her purse on her way home after collecting her pension. Mary found it and took it back.'

'And found the old lady dead?' asked Detective Sergeant Davis.

'No – she couldn't have got into the house. She obviously spent some time there – the purse was put away, her satchel was slung on the chair. The old lady must have died while the child was there. She got scared and ran off.'

'And a passing motorist knocked her down?'

'That's about it.'

'Hm. Those Flint women said she'd only a little money when

148

she bought the sweets. But there was a fifty pence piece in her pocket when she was found.'

'A reward from the old lady, perhaps.'

'Could be.' Sergeant David cogitated. 'Major Johnson?' he asked at last. 'It looks black for him, doesn't it?'

'Only for want of other evidence,' said Coward. 'I think he's a good man, in the old-fashioned sense – always lived by a strict code. An honourable man. There are a few still around. Those boys were mixed up in it somehow, I'm certain. Brewis's prints were all over the car.'

'The major seems to fancy the ladies,' said Davis mildly.

'I don't think he knows how to fancy them,' said the chief inspector. 'Or how to pick them. That one at the library must be a hard case. Do you know her?'

'I've seen her about. Nothing to look at – mousy, rather. My wife knows her – she plays in the orchestra and so does Phyllis. Bit conceited, Miss Mainwaring, Phyllis says, but with reason. Very capable – good in the library, good at the violin, and good at tennis.'

'Hm. What about human relations?'

'Likes sorting people out – telling them what to do,' said Davis. 'Or so Phyllis says.'

'Sexy?'

'Phyl wouldn't know. Want me to find out from somebody else? Someone at the tennis club? Or shall I call on her and find out for myself?'

Tension was slackening. Both men knew they were going to crack this case, and soon.

'We'll see – it may be a good idea,' said Coward. 'About the other lady – the mysterious one. How do we know it is somebody else? Major Johnson denied that it was Miss Mainwaring but he seems to have this notion that the age of chivalry is not dead.'

'She sent the plant back. Wouldn't he have told us after that, if she was the one?'

'I wonder.' The chief inspector thought for a few seconds, twiddling his biro. Then he decided. 'Let's ask the fair Celia herself. We know of no other women in the major's life. If it wasn't Celia, she may know who her rival was.'

'I'm to go myself?'

'Yes. We need a man of experience for this mission,' said Coward, grinning. 'Now, about Tom West. Young Forrest's done a good job on this one.' He tapped the report. 'Couldn't find the garage owners – they've moved away – so he tried the bank. Went round all the banks asking who used to pay the money in and do the books. Some woman working part-time. She knew Tom's name and remembered his address, from his insurance card. Forrest very sensibly didn't go barging in on top of the family, just checked they did all live at the address given – mother, father, son and two daughters. Very much respected as a family. Son's been out of work for weeks, idling about. Forrest happened to be passing Bert's Cafe on his search, so he went in and asked if Roger Brewis had been seen there lately, such as on Thursday last. He wasn't, but Tom West was, late in the evening. He was soaked through. Couple of girls were there when Forrest was asking, and they remembered. Must be the right night, because of the storm. Seems they tried to chat him up and got a dusty answer. They also said they'd seen him with Brewis at other times.'

'Forrest seems to be a promising lad,' said Davis.

'Yes. Better watch him. Too much zeal can lead to trouble,' said the chief inspector. 'Now, who was responsible for calling at *The Hollies* in the search for Mary and passed it up?'

'I've dealt with that, sir,' said Davis, and named the offending constables.

'Hm. Thought it was unnecessary to proceed further, did they? When every house and hovel in the village was to be investigated? Who were they to decide what was necessary or not?'

'Yes, sir. Exactly, sir. I told them all that,' said Davis.

'Threw it at them, did you?'

'I did, sir.'

'Want me to leave it, then?'

'Reckon I did enough,' said the sergeant.

'All right, Dick. Lucky for them I'm so busy, or they'd wish they'd never been born.' The chief inspector put his biro down and pushed his chair back. We'll go and talk to Mrs West and the enigmatic *belle dame sans merci*. Miss Mainwaring, I mean.'

'What, both of us?' Davis was grinning. The inspector only called him Dick when he felt benign and things were going well. 'I thought you wanted me to go alone.'

'I've changed my mind,' said Coward. 'That man must be in hell, though most of it's of his own causing. We'd better get our skates on. Come on. Let's go and see the lady. Now.'

VII

Roger Brewis had run out of money. He'd moved on from the hostel and spent last night sleeping rough. He'd have to do something – get some cash somehow, and then find a gang who'd let him in. It should be easy enough if he could flash the money around. On Sunday night he started prowling, looking for somewhere to break in.

As dusk was falling he wandered into a residential area on the outskirts of Liverpool. The houses were trim and expensive, most of them screened from the road by high hedges or elaborate fencing. There would be things worth taking here, if he could find an unlocked window or an open door: jewellery for sure, and with luck, cash. He circled round the deserted streets noting the lights that came on in downstairs windows as the daylight failed. The folk inside would be having their supper, settling down to the telly. He came to a house where no lights showed, opened the gate and went up the short drive and round to the back.

The top half of a window was open. Roger was able to swing himself up and reach inside to open the lower half. He climbed through, and was in a cloakroom.

He had no torch but he'd got a box of matches. By their light he groped his way upstairs to the main bedroom where he found without very much trouble a couple of rings, a watch, and a brooch. He went downstairs again and into the various rooms on the ground floor. Here he was careful not to let his flickering match shine anywhere near the uncurtained windows. There were several ornaments and figurines about the place but they were bulky to carry away and might break. However, in a desk in a book-lined room that smelled of leather and cigars he found twenty pounds in banknotes.

He felt better after that and made off quickly before his luck ran out.

Half a mile away, after several false tries, he found a house with an open door. There were some more rings there and a travelling clock. In a mug in the kitchen he found some money; not much, two pounds and a few odd pence, but it all helped. There was a pork pie and some milk in the fridge in this house, and he had a quick snack there. He took a silver cigarette-lighter, too, which he found on the sitting-room mantelpiece; it would be better for lighting his way around than the matches and he could flog it later. This was money for old rope. He'd invest in a torch for the future.

There were quite a number of houses where the people were out or away, and most were securely locked, but Roger found a third with a window open. He took a transistor radio from there; it fitted into his inner pocket. In the main bedroom a woman's handbag lay on the bed; there was a purse inside containing her generous housekeeping allowance. Roger strode away from the area with jaunty steps. Folk were stupid. He'd find some mug who'd buy the rings, and the other things; meanwhile he'd enough in hard cash to last quite a time and to flaunt about while he found some new mates.

VIII

Mrs Forman senior looked at her daughter-in-law.

'It's true then, Jean?'

Jean stared back at her, plucking nervously at the fabric of her blue cotton skirt. She shouldn't be wearing such a bright colour, she supposed, but she'd nothing black.

'It was Eileen Brown told me,' said Mrs Forman, pressing on doggedly. 'She's fond of minding everyone else's business, as you well know. So I told her it was rubbish and to watch her tongue. But I'd to find out the truth for myself. Seems she's seen you getting into this car of a Thursday after the club meetings and driving off. The young fellow that lodges at The Rising Sun, she said it is.'

Jean said nothing.

'Joe doesn't know?' The older woman's voice was not quite steady as she asked this.

'No – he hasn't a notion. He thinks I'm – I was – perfectly happy,' Jean said in a bitter voice.

'And why weren't you, with a good man and a nice home? Oh, Joe's no film star, I know that, but he's solid and decent, and that's worth more than all your glamour.'

'Joe's a good man,' Jean agreed.

'You'll not let him find out. He couldn't stand it – the shame – not on top of this other,' Mrs Forman stated. 'Young women get ideas. It'd have come to nothing. You'll not be going on with it.'

'Mrs Brown will tell him,' Jean said. She didn't care what happened. She felt utterly numb, as though nothing would ever move her again.

'I'll see to Eileen Brown,' said Mrs Forman grimly. 'You needn't fear she'll spread a tale like that abroad. I haven't known her for thirty years for nothing.' She got up. The two women had been sitting stiffly in armchairs in the sitting-room. 'I had to speak,' Mrs Forman went on. 'I'd only brood on this, else. Now's the time to clear the air. I'll never mention it again.' She paused, resting her hand lightly on Jean's shoulder. 'It made no difference to poor little Mary,' she added. 'Don't be thinking that.' At the door she turned. 'The inquest's to-morrow?'

'Yes. At the school. Eleven o'clock.'

'I'll see to dinner then. I'll make a pie. You'll both be needing something hot, after. Come round to my place when it's over.'

'You'll be there, won't you?' Jean asked.

'Oh yes. They may want to ask about Mary coming to see me that afternoon. We'll sit together, Jean,' Mrs Forman said. 'There'll be no talk.'

IX

The library did not open on Mondays. This suited Celia Mainwaring. She was usually out most of the weekend, with various friends or playing tennis, which went on throughout the year since the Leckington Club had three quick-drying hard courts. So on Mondays she did odd jobs at home – not much cleaning, for a woman came in three times a week to deal with that – but she went to the launderette and she had a shampoo and set at three o'clock every week. After that she had tea at The Hazel Nut, where she always found at least one acquaintance.

She was about to set forth for her hair appointment when Chief Inspector Coward and Detective Sergeant Davis rang her bell.

'Miss Celia Mainwaring?' Coward eyed her with interest when she opened the door. She was small, about five foot three inches tall, and quite curvy, but at first glance she seemed to him to be totally without the elusive quality he and the sergeant had been discussing.

Celia knew at once that they were policemen.

'Yes?' she said in a frosty voice.

'I am Chief Inspector Coward and this is Detective Sergeant Davis. We'd just like a word or two with you, if we might come in for a moment. We won't keep you long.'

What could they want? She would have to admit them. Celia led the way into her sitting-room and sat down in a Victorian button-back chair, upholstered in turquoise velvet.

'Sit down, inspector – sergeant – ' Celia said, drawing her pleated grey skirt down over her knees. Coward saw Davis wink at him slightly as they lowered themselves on to a knoll-type settee covered in yellow damask.

'What a charming room,' said Coward, looking about him.

It was. Celia's mother had had excellent taste and had been left a modest but adequate income when her husband was killed during the war. She had come to Leckington then, as it was an area away from likely bombing targets, and had found this small house in a quiet cul-de-sac. A doll's house, she'd called it.

'I'm glad you think so,' said Celia. She looked at her watch pointedly. 'Now, what can I do for you, Inspector? I have an appointment in ten minutes' time.'

Coward decided to go straight to the point.

'You are acquainted, I believe, with Major Frederick Johnson, of *Tobruk*, Wiveldown,' he said.

Miss Mainwaring stiffened.

'He comes to the library,' she said.

'Ah – a business relationship?' said Coward.

'That is all,' said Celia.

'Yet I understand he sent you a gift?'

'He had the effrontery to send me a potted plant. I returned it,' said Celia coldly.

'Oh, why? Wasn't it, perhaps, an expression of gratitude?'

'For what?'

'Services given,' said the chief inspector, and Sergeant Davis took out his handkerchief to mop at his nose.

'My acquaintance with Major Johnson was strictly limited to library hours,' said Miss Mainwaring firmly.

'But you'd been helpful to him at the library? Taken trouble to find him particular books?'

'No more than any other subscriber,' said Celia. 'I enjoy my work and try to do it conscientiously.'

'And don't some of your readers appreciate it, and give you occasional tokens of esteem?'

'At Christmas, occasionally.' There had been some home-made fudge once, she remembered; no more. 'Not flowers – from male readers,' she said in a voice charged with outrage.

'Well, then – I take it you did not invite Major Johnson to a meal here with you on Thursday evening?'

'Certainly not! Why? Does he say that I did?'

'No – not at all. But we believe he dined with a lady that night and we don't know who. You have no idea, I suppose?'

'I do not,' said Celia. 'And now, if you'll excuse me – '

'Just a moment, Miss Mainwaring. Why wouldn't you keep the plant?'

'I have no wish to be mixed up with that man,' she said.

'But why? Has he ever insulted you? Or made an improper suggestion to you?'

'No, not at all. I wouldn't permit such a thing,' said Celia.

'You lunched with him last Thursday.'

For a fraction of time Celia's poise wavered.

'I could hardly avoid it, without making a scene. He waited for me at the library and almost insisted. He seemed friendless so I took pity on him.'

'I see. You know of no other women friends he might have?'

'No. But I am not his keeper. Oh – ' she hesitated.

'Yes?'

'He sells tickets at Chorlbury Manor sometimes. Mrs Fellowes – Ruth Fellowes – she lives in Wiveldown too – they are acquainted with one another. But hardly friends, I imagine. Mrs Fellowes gives cooking lessons and Major Johnson attended a course last winter.'

'Ah yes. Her address, please?'

Celia supplied it.

'And now I must go,' she said.

They drove her to the hairdresser's, since they had made her late. She bustled into the shop without a backward glance. How right she had been to return the flowers; the very fact that the police were enquiring about Major Johnson showed how undesirable a character he must be.

'None,' said Davis, shaking his head as they watched her walk into the shop. 'All the equipment, but none of the magic.'

'Odd, isn't it?' remarked Coward. 'A worthy woman, too, in the world's eye as well as her own. But clearly a perpetual virgin.'

X

Like Roger's mother, Mrs West knew Chief Inspector Coward by sight, but she had never spoken to him. She felt slightly sick when he asked for Tom.

'He hasn't been working lately, I believe,' said Coward.

'He's got a job now, down at Walter's, the paint factory. Started today,' she said quickly.

'Ah.'

'He's not in trouble, is he?' she asked, unable to conceal her anxiety. 'He's always been a good boy – never been in trouble.' She clasped her hands together.

'We're not sure, Mrs West. That's what we have to find out,' said the chief inspector. 'Do you know what he was doing last Thursday?'

'That was the day there was that bad thunderstorm. No, I don't know where he was.'

'You remember it was the day of the storm. Now, why?'

'Well, you do remember things, don't you? And besides –' she stopped.

'Well?'

'Tom got soaked through,' she said lamely. 'But anyone would, out in that lot.'

'You've washed his clothes, of course?' Mrs West had been ironing when they called, and a neat pile of clean washing was stacked on the kitchen table.

'Yes.' She gestured at the heap of laundry. Some faded jeans could be seen.

'What about his shoes?'

'He had a pair of plimsolls on. Those rubber things. He's got them on today.'

'What time did he come home on Thursday, after the storm?'

'Not all that late. Midnight, maybe,' said Mrs West.

'Or later?'

'Could have been. I didn't look at the time.'

No, thought the policeman, but you listened for him. You were anxious.

'I see. And who are his friends now, Mrs West?'

'I don't know. He used to go to the youth club. They'd tell you. But he hasn't been there lately. He'll go again now he's in work.'

'Did he know a boy called Roger Brewis?'

'I don't know,' said Mrs West again, but her face went pale. 'That's the boy you're looking for. Oh, Tom wouldn't know him.' Now she looked really frightened.

'Leckington's not a big town. They're of an age. Probably they do know each other, Mrs West.'

'Yes, but not to be friendly. He wouldn't be mixed up in anything, would Tom.' But he'd been in a terrible state of nerves these past few days. If he'd seen Roger – no, it wasn't thinkable.

'Brewis has disappeared. Your Tom might be able to help us find him – that's all,' said Coward. 'I'll see him some other time and find out where he was on Thursday. Thank you, Mrs West.'

He went back to join Detective Sergeant Davis, who had waited in the car in case Tom, if at home, had tried to get away from the house. As the sergeant slid the car into gear and moved off down the road, the chief inspector sighed.

'This is when I hate our job, Dick. What a nice, respectable woman.'

'We don't know that young West was involved.'

'No – but he was seen with Brewis in the market. And there are all those dabs in the car. Some may be his.' In a way he hoped so, for the major's sake.

'Are we going to the paint works now?'

'No. We'll wait for the boy. Or rather, you will. Take young Forrest with you, let him meet his prey. Bring the boy in and treat him gently. And get a print – the cup of tea method, for choice.'

'Let him go, then?'

'Unless he asks to stay, yes, this time.'

XI

While Sergeant Davis and Constable Forrest made their plans to meet Tom West on his way home from work, Chief Inspector Coward went out to Wiveldown again. He found Ruth Fellowes' cottage and soon discovered that she was out, so he took an exploratory prowl round her garden. The road below was invisible and he could not see even the roof of his car, which he had left close to the side of the road. Thoughtfully, he walked back to it.

The stolen bicycles had been found not far from here. He drove to the spot and stood in the road meditating. Then he got back into his car and drove slowly back towards Ruth's cottage. In all this time nothing had passed that way.

He parked once more outside Ruth's gate and walked slowly along towards the village. There were hedges on both sides of the road, cleanly cut-and-laid the year before but sprouting strongly now; a mechanical cutter would trim them next time. Less than a hundred yards beyond the cottage he saw a gap in the hedge filled by a stile. Beyond was a field with some cattle in it.

Coward climbed the stile and walked some distance over the field. In places it was still damp and the mud stuck to his shoes.

He went back to the police station and pored over a map, plotting Mary's possible movements when she left *The Hollies*, while a constable went down to the laboratory with a generous supply of mud from the Wiveldown field.

Mrs Eileen Brown was having a cup of tea with her friend Cassie Castle.

'And there he stood, right in Mr Duckett's shop as large as life, and he'd do you or me in next, as like as not,' she said. 'I can tell you, it made my flesh creep. He shouldn't be let out, that's what,' she added, with a delighted shudder.

'You think he did it, then?' Mrs Castle did not form her opinions with the same haste as her friend.

'Who else?' demanded Mrs Brown. 'He was going to bury poor little Mary in his garden, by dead of night, but it was too wet on Thursday, and on Friday it was full moon. Someone might have seen.'

'Oh, Eileen, I don't know. He never did it, surely.'

'Who else?' Mrs Brown asked for the second time. 'I've always thought him a strange one. Them eyes. They kind of look through you.'

Mrs Castle was not sure if she had ever seen the major. She had certainly not gazed into his eyes.

'And living alone like that. It's not natural,' Mrs Brown went on.

'Folk do. The vicar. And Mr Bellings.'

Mr Bellings was a widower, like the vicar, and he lived near Mrs Forman senior in a council bungalow.

'They were both married. Poor Bertha.'

'Yes.'

Both ladies were silent for some seconds in tribute to bad-tempered Bertha Bellings, long deceased, whose bereaved husband was now one of the happiest members of the Darby and Joan club, where ladies outnumbered gentleman by four to one. He was invited out to Sunday dinner regularly by the various widowed ladies whom he met there, and his life was a great deal pleasanter now than it had been when Bertha kept at him for making marks on all her floors, and made him wear a collar and tie on Sundays.

'The children, Cassie. We must think of all the children,'

Eileen said. 'Your grandchildren. My grandchildren. What about them, with that monster free among us? I've told our Ivy not to let them out until he's put away.' Ivy was Mrs Brown's daughter, mother of three tough little boys all rather like their grandmother.

Cassie's grandchildren were still in their prams, so she felt unaffected at the moment. The two women had lived in the district for their whole lives; their fathers had worked on the land, and they had married local men who had begun their working lives as farm labourers, but now Eileen's husband worked for a haulage firm, and Cassie's drove a van for the local water board.

'Let's go down there, Cassie, and tell him what we think of him,' said Eileen.

'What – Major Johnson? You mean talk to him?'

'Well – let's see if he's there. If he sees how we feel, maybe he'll give himself up.'

'Oh, I don't know, Eileen.'

'He wouldn't meet my eye, in Duckett's shop,' insisted Eileen, who had kept hers so averted from the major's contaminating gaze that he could not have done so if he tried. 'If he'd been innocent, he would of.'

'Well, I'm not sure.'

'You're scared,' taunted Eileen.

'No – no, I'm not.' Eileen was always so impetuous. 'We could walk down and have a look, at least. There'd be no harm in that,' Cassie allowed.

'Right, then,' said Eileen promptly. As they walked down the path she picked up two or three stones, each nearly the size of a golf ball, and put them in the pocket of her shapeless cardigan. Cassie, alarmed, pretended not to see.

They started down the road. On the way they met some friends, and their ranks swelled when Eileen explained where they were going.

'Just to have a look,' Cassie kept insisting. 'Not to talk to him.'

By the time they reached the church there were ten of them,

all middle-aged, some uncertain why they'd come but all convinced by now that the major couldn't be 'quite right'.

The bungalow looked peaceful in the evening light, with the sinking sun casting a rosy glow above the major's garage. Shadows stretched across his front lawn.

'That's where she was,' said Mrs Brown. 'Poor Mary, stiff and cold in that garridge. All those hours, there she lay.' She was quoting from the press.

A woman gave a sob.

'While Jean and Joe were hunting high and low for her,' Eileen went on, not quite accurately, since Jean had never left the house.

'And all our men.'

That was true. Almost every able-bodied man had joined the search parties.

'Murderer,' hissed Eileen Brown, and one of the other women repeated it.

They began to chant.

'Murderer! Murderer! Give yourself up! Come out and give yourself up!'

From inside the bungalow came an odd, deep booming sound. It was the major's trombone.

XIII

Cathy and Derek were having a row when the mournful sound of the major's trombone came wafting to them over the garden.

When Derek got home from work, Cathy told him that she meant to invite the major to supper the next evening, after the inquest.

'I forbid you to do it. We don't want people to think we're friends with a man like that,' said Derek.

'Why not? I am friends with him,' said Cathy defiantly. 'He's a nice, harmless old man.'

162

'He's mixed up in this terrible business. It could ditch my chances of promotion if I'm involved too,' said Derek.

'Well, you are involved already. You were there when Mary was found.'

'That was just an accident,' said Derek.

'You'll have to go to the inquest, won't you? You can't dodge that,' Cathy said. 'You can't seriously think the major had anything to do with it, Derek.'

'I don't know what to think. People just don't go round with bodies in the boots of their cars,' said Derek. 'Until the police have sorted it all out I'm not having anything to do with Major Johnson, and neither are you. In fact, even if there is some sort of explanation that absolves him, I'm not sure – anyway, we don't know how it will go.'

'What do you mean?' Cathy asked him.

'I don't like solitary old men who make a habit of talking to little children – boys or girls,' said Derek. He suddenly looked so obstinate that Cathy's heart sank. Where was the kind man she thought she had married?

'You're condemning him before any court has done it,' she said in a very quiet voice.

'I don't think it's healthy,' Derek insisted.

'And what if the vicar talks to little boys or girls? Is he a pervert too? Is there no relationship that isn't suspect?'

'Oh, of course there is. Don't twist my words,' said Derek angrily.

'And don't you try to twist my mind,' said Cathy, just as violently. 'I shall ask him here tomorrow night.'

'And if you do, I shall refuse to have him in the house,' said Derek.

They stared at each other, both suddenly terrified by the enormous chasm that had opened up between them. Into the silence that fell came the notes of the trombone.

'Whatever's that?' cried Derek, thankful for the diversion.

Cathy was bewildered at first, but then she realised what it was.

'Major Johnson played in a military band when he was young. It's his trombone, I expect,' she said.

163

'I've never heard it before,' said Derek.

'No. He only plays when everyone's out,' said Cathy. 'He told me so.'

'I wonder why he's playing it now,' said Derek.

The windows of their house were open and the sound had drifted through. He walked out on to the flagged terrace and listened. Cathy followed. She was trembling, but she knew she must stick to her views or she would betray herself as well as the major.

They heard the bass notes, slow and ponderous. Then the noise altered, and another sound, less hesitant, came to them. It was the chant of voices.

They could not make out what was being said. The trombone had ceased, and Derek began to walk towards his gate, trying to catch what the voices shouted.

'Murderer! Murderer!' he heard, and Cathy, following, heard it too.

'Give yourself up! Give yourself up! Murderer!' came the cry, as Derek went into the road.

The women were standing on the pavement outside the major's bungalow, shaking their fists and shouting. Cathy and Derek looked at one another in horror, and as Derek stood there hesitating, the first stone was thrown, shattering the glass in the major's front door.

'Go and ring the police, quick. I'll stop them,' Derek said, striding forward.

Cathy paused long enough to see him raise an arm to shield his face from another stone as he moved into the group; then she fled back into her own house.

XIV

Tom did not know that Joe Forman worked at the paint factory. He was sweeping out the yard under the direction of an elderly man whose job it was to keep the stores and surrounding area tidy, when two men walked past.

164

'That's Joe Forman. Chap whose little girl got killed last week,' said Tom's superior.

'What? Who? Where?' Tom started and stared at the men.

'Him on the left. Poor bugger,' said the old man. 'Nice little kiddie, she was. Used to come on the works outings and to social club parties sometimes. Bad business, that. Papers seem to think that Major Johnson was responsible. He worked here too, once.'

Tom was gazing at Joe's retreating back. All he saw was a stocky shape in overalls, with dark hair and a small balding patch.

'Oh! Did he?' Tom said.

Ten minutes later, Joe, alone, returned through the yard, and Tom saw his face: pale, rather lined. Not a young man any more.

' 'Morning, Bill,' he said to Tom's boss, and Bill went to talk to him. While they conversed quietly together Tom swept his way industriously out of earshot. He had caught Mary's name being mentioned. It wasn't just her death for which he was to blame, but also for the grief of this man who was not unlike Tom's own father. The full extent of the horror of his act at last began to register.

He worked zealously throughout the day, for by heaving heavy boxes around and leaping to the bidding of Bill, he was able to thrust it all out of his mind for a time, but the end of the day came at last when he had to stop this activity.

'You and me'll get along, young Tom, I can tell,' said Bill approvingly, thumping him on the back. 'Quite a worker, you are. See you tomorrow, lad.'

Tom nodded and managed a smile.

He walked home thinking of Joe Forman, and thinking too about Major Johnson, who had done nothing wrong but who had become, like Mary, a sort of victim. Bit of an old fogey, he'd seemed, but he'd listened to Tom's request for work very civilly.

It was all Roger's fault. He'd been behind the whole thing – the stealing of the boots, the drinking, the lot.

But Tom had driven the car.

Of course they wouldn't clobber the major for it. The fuzz would know he hadn't done it. The thing was to play it cool and in the end it'd all blow over. Roger would keep away, that was for sure, and good riddance too. All he, Tom, must do was keep his nerve.

He was thinking along these lines when he turned into his own street and saw the police car. It began to move slowly towards him as he approached. He kept his eyes fixed on the road ahead and tried to ignore it, but it was hopeless; he kept glancing at it. And he hadn't the heart to run; what would be the point?

I won't admit a thing, he vowed. They can't make me. He kept telling himself this as he allowed Detective Sergeant Davis and Constable Forrest to take him off to police headquarters.

XV

Derek had witnessed mob violence when he was a student, but he had never before seen middle-aged women lose control and he was revolted. Until he saw their faces contorted with hysteria he had to some extent sympathised with the viewpoint of these women, but this conduct was primitive. He sought for a face he recognised, and saw one: Mrs Castle, who for a time had helped behind the bar at The Rising Sun.

'Mrs Castle,' he thundered. 'Stop that at once,' and at the same time he grabbed the arm of the woman nearest to him and pulled her back from Major Johnson's fence.

Cassie, who had stifled her earlier doubts and was shouting as loudly as anyone, hesitated and took a backward step; the woman Derek had seized fell silent from sheer surprise. Derek elbowed his way past them and reached the gate, which Mrs Brown had been about to open. He interposed his own body between it and her.

'Go back to your homes immediately,' he commanded.

The chanting dribbled to a halt, and the women gaped at him; then they looked at each other, some of them seeking guidance but others feeling sheepish. Derek tried to think of a telling remark to make but failed. Attack was the best method of defence, so he rounded on Mrs Brown.

'You threw that stone. You'll be liable for damages,' he snarled at her. 'What's your name?'

Mrs Brown did not answer. She was trying to summon up her reserves for a counter-attack.

'Never mind. I won't forget you. You'll pay all right, I'll see to that,' he said. 'And you'll be prosecuted too, if I have my way.' He glared round at them all. 'The lot of you will,' he threatened.

At this even Eileen Brown's belligerence faltered. Cassie pulled at her arm.

'We'd better go,' she said. 'Come on, Eileen. We've had our say.'

They began to disperse, shuffling off down the road, some looking rather abashed but a few still angry.

'Who's he think he is?' demanded Eileen Brown. 'Have the law on us, indeed? The law should do its own job, that's what.' She continued to mutter, but she moved away.

When he saw that they were really going, Derek went up the path to the door of the bungalow. He put his hand through the broken glass and opened it. Major Johnson was sitting in the living-room with his head bowed forward, his face in his hands, staring at the floor. The trombone lay at his feet.

The two constables in their Panda car who came in response to Cathy's telephone call met the little band of no-longer-militant women moving away up the road, and they found Derek still staring at the major, who had not moved nor spoken since he entered the bungalow.

PART FIVE

I

THE NEWSPAPERS were quick to exploit this new turn of events. There was a dearth of political drama that week, and they were featuring the Forman case in detail since they had space to fill. An alert reporter saw the Panda car hurrying out to Wiveldown and soon discovered what had happened.

Ruth's hostess, in Tenby, read the news to her at breakfast.

'I see the villagers where you live have been taking the law into their own hands,' she remarked. 'That man must be mixed up in it somehow, in spite of what you say.' For they had already discussed the tragedy, though Ruth had not been very forthcoming about it.

'Of course he isn't. He wouldn't hurt a fly – unless it threatened Queen or country,' Ruth said.

'Where was he, then, on Thursday night?' Ruth's friend demanded.

'What? Here – let me look!' Ruth snatched the paper from the other woman and learned from it that Major Johnson's car had been seen returning late on the night of the incident, when he had alleged he was at home. 'Oh no! Oh, how could he be so foolish!' Ruth exclaimed, half to herself. 'I must ring up the police at once,' she told her friend.

Detective Chief Inspector Coward arrived at *Tobruk* soon after half-past nine on Tuesday morning. Major Johnson was wearing a dark suit and a black tie, in readiness for the inquest. He was pale, and all the lines on his face sagged downwards; in two days he had aged ten years. A pile of letters, not all of them opened, lay on the table in his sitting-room, and the telephone was off the hook.

'Hm – more letters, I see,' said Coward. 'And you've had phone calls, too, have you?'

'Yes.'

Major Johnson had slept very little during the night. A police guard had remained outside the bungalow, and there had been no more trouble from the village, but it had taken him some time to think of leaving the telephone receiver off.

'Well, your worries are over now,' Coward said. He felt expansive. 'I should burn that lot.' He waved his hand at the letters. 'We've got it wrapped up now. But you should have telephoned, yesterday, when those women came round. You could have had protection sooner.'

Major Johnson laughed shortly.

'British justice,' he said. 'Mob law.'

'People behave strangely at these times,' said Coward. 'That Mrs Brown, the ringleader – termagant type.' He was pleased with the word, and said it again. 'A termagant. Do you want to bring a case against her? You'd be within your rights.'

'What good would it do?' asked Major Johnson. 'The harm's been done. But you know what happened, do you?' He'd almost stopped caring by this time.

'We do. We've got the two boys concerned – the pair who stole the bicycles. Roger Brewis was picked up in Liverpool yesterday. He'd been trying to sell stolen property. He'd broken into several houses on Sunday night – left fingerprints all over the place – there's no doubt about his identity. He's on his way back here now, to be charged.'

'With what?'

'Stealing a bicycle and a pair of boots to start with. Another boy actually drove your car, but we believe Brewis was the ring-leader. Tom West's the other lad. He was the one who killed Mary Forman.'

'She was killed with my car?'

'Young West admitted everything last night, when he heard Brewis had been caught. They saw your car in Lammas Lane

170

on Thursday night and took it to get home, having ditched the two bicycles they'd stolen earlier. They'd made a day of it – pinched some drink and lain up in a barn at Mordwell knocking it back. West knew how to start a car without the key – bragged about it – he'd worked at a garage, though only on the pumps. They'd gone a hundred yards or so when Mary suddenly appeared in front of them – she came through a gap in the fence – there's a stile there. They never saw her. You'd think she'd have heard them, but she'd had a fright – she may have run out in front of the car intending to stop it.' He told Major Johnson about Mrs Pollock. 'When the boys found Mary was dead they put her in the boot of your car and took it back to where they'd found it. Brewis disappeared and left young West to face the music on his own. He came to see you on Sunday. Curious to know what you were like. Troubled with his conscience.'

'What? That boy with all the hair?' The one he'd thought a civil lad.

'That's right. He met Joe Forman, too – brought it all home to him. He'd have given himself up pretty soon if we hadn't got on to him – couldn't have stood it.'

Major Johnson was silent.

'What will happen to him?' he asked.

'Probably have to face a manslaughter charge,' said Coward. 'And of course driving without a licence and all that.'

'Prison, then?'

'Certainly. There's all the thieving too.'

'And the other boy? You say it was all his fault?'

'Yes – but he wasn't driving the car. He's got a record, though, and a lot to answer for up in Liverpool.'

'Young West doesn't seem very good at choosing his friends,' said the major slowly. 'He's a victim of circumstance, like me.'

'You'd have saved yourself – and us – a good deal of trouble if you'd told us where you were on Thursday night,' pointed out the chief inspector.

'You seem to have discovered anyway.'

'West told us where the car was. And Mrs Fellowes telephoned just before I left the station this morning. She'd read about the women molesting you and all that.'

Molesting. So that was what it was.

'Why didn't you tell us about her, Major?'

'I saw no reason why she should be involved,' said Major Johnson austerely. 'I knew the child's death was not of my direct doing, and that you'd find out the truth eventually.'

'Yes – but at what a cost,' said Coward. In a way the man was ridiculous, yet somehow this attitude impressed.

'It was my fault that Mary died,' said Major Johnson. 'I was to blame.'

'You weren't, Major.'

'I couldn't have locked my car. I am always most particular about locking it, but that night it was raining hard and I must have been careless. The boys wouldn't have taken it if it had been locked.'

'They might have. Young West would have opened it. He'd have boasted to Brewis that he could and been forced to prove it, to save his face.'

'Then it would have taken longer, and Mary would have escaped, perhaps,' said Major Johnson. He shook his head. 'Those poor people, the Formans. Perhaps Mary did try to get a lift. I told her that afternoon that she shouldn't hitch-hike. She said she was doing it to save her bus fare.'

'Mrs Fellowes was on the two o'clock bus that day. She said you passed her while she was waiting at the stop. Why didn't you pick her up too?'

The major looked surprised.

'I never noticed her. We're just acquaintances, you know, that's all, but she's been kind. I gave her a lift home that night because of the storm, and she invited me to supper.'

'So she said.' Poor old fool, thought Coward, fantasising about the proud librarian when all the time there was this widow on his doorstep; she'd been very concerned about him on the telephone and said she was coming home at once. Coward decided not to impart this piece of news. 'Well, there's a neat report for the coroner – everything cut and dried, with no loose ends,' he said.

'I'm to attend the inquest?'

'Yes, please. Just a formality – you may not be called.'

'And Mrs Pollock?'

'Oh – that's a separate matter. No problems there.'

Except for his negligent constables.

II

The inquest did not take long. The school was packed, and the silent spectators heard a verdict of accidental death returned. They trooped out of the building talking in hushed voices, some still very shocked by what had happened, but a few with blunted sensibilities feeling a sense of anti-climax. There was no lurid murder after all.

The vicar drove the Formans home and went in with them to talk about the funeral, which could now be planned. Miss Price walked along the road, wheeling her bicycle, talking to Joe's mother. Derek hurried back to his office, and everyone else dispersed in various directions. No one gave a thought to Major Johnson.

He went home and wrote two letters. One he put on his sitting-room mantelpiece, underneath his gleaming bugle, the other he took immediately to the letter-box on the corner near the vicarage. He met no one on this excursion.

His telephone was still off the hook and he did not put it back. Cathy had been trying to get through to him with her invitation for the evening but had got no reply, so she intended to call in later in the day.

To his surprise, Major Johnson felt hungry, so he cooked some of the food he had bought at Duckett's the day before. Then he sat at his window watching until Cathy went past wheeling the pram. On Tuesday afternoons he knew she took the baby to the clinic and would be out for an hour or so.

When she had gone by he went out into the garden and walked around it. He had achieved something in claiming it back from the wilderness it had been, but it was not enough to comfort him now. His integrity had been questioned and found wanting, and he saw no end to loneliness ahead. He was of use to no one any longer.

Inspector Coward would get his letter in the morning. It was unfortunate that he would cause more trouble, but his affairs were all in order. He hoped the rough will he had made would be valid; his possessions would be scant compensation to the Formans for the loss of Mary, but if they sold the bungalow they would raise enough to start up some small business of their own, in another area, perhaps.

There was no one within earshot. On Tuesdays Mrs Philpot played golf in the morning and bridge in the afternoons, so she was not at home, and her husband would be at his butcher's shop.

Major Johnson went back into the bungalow. He took the bugle down from the wall and gave it a rub on the sleeve of his jacket. Then he opened his desk and took out his service revolver. In the same drawer was his row of medals, just service ones, no special awards for valour or for duty done. He gave them a glance and closed the drawer again.

He thought for a moment as he sat down in his armchair of his companions in the army; of the sense of comradeship; the heat and dust of the desert; the calmer, postwar life. There were tasks for every day.

Then, holding his bugle tightly in his left hand, with his other hand he raised the revolver to his head and shot himself.

Other bestselling Warner titles available by mail: